D0206849

Queen of Someday

A Stolen Empire Novel

Sherry Ficklin

Clean Teen Publishing

QUEEN OF *Someday*

ISBN: 978-1-940534-90-9
Cover Design by: Marya Heiman
Typography by: Courtney Nuckels
Editing by: Cynthia Shepp

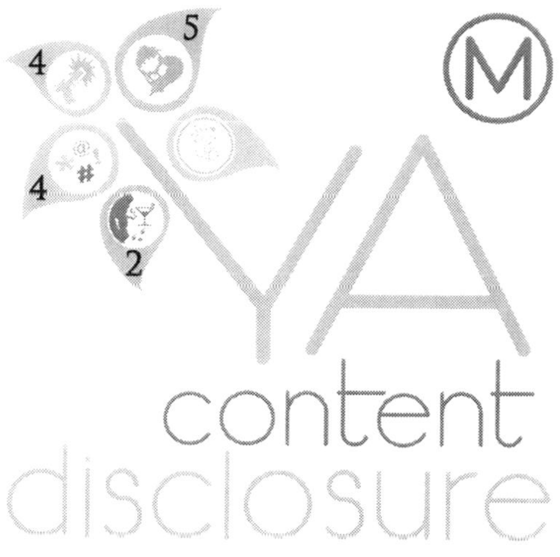

For more information about our content disclosure, please utilize the QR code above with your smart phone or visit us at

www.CleanTeenPublishing.com.

For all you hardworking history teachers who want to hit me with a book after reading this. The line forms here. No pushing. Everyone will get a turn.

Prologue

And then he does the most dangerous, reckless thing he ever could have done.

He kisses me.

The moment our lips touch, the last fraying strands of my self-control snap and I reach up, clasping my hands behind his neck and pulling him against me. There's no reason, no judgment—only gentle waves of relief. I'm lost in the ocean of his embrace, drowning in him. I could live a hundred lifetimes inside his kiss, and it would never be enough. One single thought surfaces through the tide of emotions.

"Of the entire universe, I only wanted you," I whisper the words against his lips, a solemn pledge.

His hands slide up my back and into my hair, working it loose with his fingers until it falls in brown waves across my shoulders. I sigh against his mouth and he responds by pulling away just a bit, laying a kiss on the tip of my nose, my forehead, and beside my eye, before returning to my lips.

"You have ruined me," he whispers against my mouth, his voice thick with desire.

Chapter One

The sled is cramped; my legs and back ache in protest as we cut through the deep snow. I pull back the heavy damask curtain covering the small window. Outside the landscape is barren and desolate. Nothing but stark white snow for miles, interrupted by the occasional leafless tree. Though the horses race forward across the plain as fast as they are able, the trek has been long and the snow deep so they snort with exertion. We'd had to abandon our more spacious carriage in Livonia and continue the rest of the way in this small sled. Across from me, my mother carefully stitches on her small linen even as each bump threatens to destroy the colorful tapestry she's creating. She hasn't spoken to me in two days, not since I'd finally grown weary of her constant chatter about how different and lavish life would be at a *real* court and reprimanded her harshly.

I sigh deeply. Perhaps the rolling hills of Anhault-Zerbst are not as grand as the palaces of Berlin, where she grew up in the home of our wealthiest aunt, but it was my father's land and my only home. Never have I missed it more than I do on this journey, the dangerous trek through the depths of Russia in the coldest months of winter. I have acquired a constant shiver and my toes and fingers never seem to thaw. Still, it was only Mother's callous remarks about my father that had provoked me to speak rudely to her, and she is making me pay for it now, making the already cold interior of the carriage seem absolutely frigid with her indifference.

Letting the heavy damask curtain fall back into place, I sit back, stretching beneath the thick, fur blanket heaped over my legs. Closing my eyes, I rest against the seat, and I can almost feel the warm summer sun on my face. Days of running through the field with my darling little brother and sister, as we chased down chickens that had escaped the coop, float through my mind like soap bubbles. I remember sitting on the edge of the creek for hours, slipping off my shoes, letting my toes soak in the water. And sometimes Gretchen, my good friend, would come and bring flowers to weave into my dark hair or a flask of wine from her father's stock for us to drink until our heads were light as a feather. It never mattered much to me that she was the daughter of the local innkeeper and I was the daughter of the prince. We were innocent of such things, much to my mother's chagrin. I can't help but smile at the memories. As they come, I try to hold them close, weaving them around me like the fragile threads under my mother's fingers.

Such happier times, though not so long ago, seem to me now as if they occurred in another lifetime.

Everything changed when I turned fourteen. Though still a girl by any accounts, Mother was desperate to see me wed. I didn't learn until much later of our family's dire financial situation, or that Father was in danger of forfeiting his family properties.

She had first tried to wed me to young Peter, then heir to the Swiss throne. But when he abdicated to move to Russia with his aunt, all hope of that union seemed lost. Mother had been forced to offer me to my uncle, an old man with missing teeth and thin, white hair. He'd come for a visit that summer and while I had thought it an innocent visit, his intentions toward me became painfully obvious. I can still remember the stench of brandy and tobacco on his breath as he'd cornered me one evening and forced a kiss upon me.

It had taken all my will not to retch on his golden slippers.

I cried into my pillow all night when Mother told me he asked for my hand in marriage. I screamed, raged, and begged—something that did not bode well in her eyes. When the letter arrived from Empress Elizabeth of Russia, we had both been deeply relieved to say the least. I cling to that feeling now, as we trek across the tundra, snow falling all around us.

Finally, after what feels like hours, I sit forward.

I'm so desperate for conversation that I ask the only question that I think might appeal to my stoic mother.

"Mother, tell me, how long do you think we are to remain at the Winter Palace?"

Her eyes flicker up to me, sparkling. She is beautiful, for all her flaws of character. Her hair is brown like mine, and perfectly smooth. Her skin is a pale crème like fresh milk, and her eyes are wide and dark blue like a storm at sea. There is absolutely nothing that makes her happier than planning what, in her mind, will be a fine royal union, and that happiness makes her even lovelier. As she answers, I would swear she is actually glowing.

"If I have my way, you will never step foot on Prussian soil again," she answers confidently. "Empress Consort," she muses wistfully, "just as I should have been."

I wish I could share her enthusiasm. Gretchen's warm smile and twinkling laugh invade my thoughts once more, and I have to force them away. It won't do to dwell on those childhood memories now. Not when my mother has made my options very clear.

"It's not an engagement," I say softly. "Not officially."

Empress Elizabeth's letter had been vague at best. A simple invitation for my mother and me to join her at Russian Court. There was not even a hint of what my mother longed for so desperately—a marriage between myself and Peter, once heir to Sweden and now the future King of Russia. Still, Mother packed us up immediately and we made for St. Petersburg even through the blistering winter, hoping to make our arrival by Peter's sixteenth birthday.

"Not yet, perhaps. But the empress favors our family—my family, that is—and she knows the best way to secure her throne is by securing her bloodline. And for that, she needs not only Peter as heir, but for Peter himself to have an heir. And for that, she will need you."

Or another princess. I don't say the words, but they buzz in my head like honeybees. The prince's birthday celebration is sure to be filled with eligible ladies from every corner of the kingdom, each vying for a place beside him. I myself have met Peter only once, when we were ten years old. He was bratty and insufferable as all boys are, but even at that age, he had subtle nobility about him, a tilt of the chin, and a confidence in his gait that only royals possess.

Deep in the back of my mind, I couldn't help but wonder what sort of man Peter had become. Is he kind? Handsome? Strong? Wise? In my mind, I allow a vague image of him to form. Surely, he would be handsome, as were the other men in his family. And even in the remote area of my home, word of his skill in the hunt and his predilection for archery were well known. Certainly, he will be a good husband and a fair and just king.

While I daydream, Mother begins to drone on about the lavish balls that we will attend, and the frivolous and silly-sounding customs I will be expected to learn to fit in at Royal Court. I lay my head back gently as she speaks, the sound of her voice soothing after such a long silence. The sled bucks and I fly forward into her lap, spilling the contents of her sewing basket.

"What in the world?" she demands as I right myself. "Why have we stopped?"

I draw back the curtain and our escort, General Pitankin, rides past the window, his chestnut mare jerking the reins skittishly.

"Stay inside," he commands.

My mother grabs a dainty, blue fan from the seat beside her and begins fanning herself despite the cold.

"I'm sure it's just beggars. I believe these woods are filled with them," she offers as if to console me.

Outside, the general yells something in Russian. I curse myself mentally. If only I had thought to learn Russian along with French and German, I wouldn't feel quite so foreign now. Still, if Mother is successful in her ambitions, I will learn the language soon enough.

There are sounds of a scuffle, and the unmistakable ring of a steel blade being drawn from its sheath. The sled rocks sideways as someone knocks into it. Mother lets out a startled squeal. I lean forward, peeking out the curtain, and see the general and another of our guards on the ground, unmoving. Quickly, I lift the hem of my brown, wool gown and slip a knife from my boot. Mother opens her mouth, I'm sure to chastise me for such an unladylike thing as having a knife hidden on my person, but I silence her with a finger to my lips. While my mother had been determined to groom me to be a proper lady, my father was content to let me join him in hunting, fencing, and even knife throwing. The small blade in my hand is one of many he's gifted me over the years, and the hilt is warm and comforting in my palm.

The sled rocks again, and I hear the stomp of boots as the thieves begin pulling our trunks from the back. They won't find any riches, only recently altered dresses and sturdy undergarments we've brought with us. Any jewels Mother might have brought are most likely hidden down the front of her corset—and there would be few of those at that. Despite being the ruler of our province, my father has no kingly riches. Our wealth lies in our title alone—a fact Mother never allows him to forget.

Soon, they are muttering in disappointed tones. I know they will come for us next; there is nothing left for them now but to amuse themselves with us. Nodding to Mother, who looks like she's about to faint, I quietly slip out of the opposite side of the sled and slink around its wooden bow, knife in hand. Snow crunches beneath my boots, but the restless stomping of the horses obscures it. I know I'm no match for them on fair terms, but if I can surprise them, then we have a chance of escape.

I see two pairs of legs standing beside the sled. Then I hear the door fly open, and my mother screams. Lunging forward, I slice into the first thief's thigh, high up where I know the blood will flow too quickly to stop. The knife is sharp enough that it takes him a moment to realize what's happening. Climbing to my feet, I lunge at the next man, who is much quicker than I hoped, and he waves off my attack. I spin, a move I've practiced more than once with the butcher's children when we used to play wooden swords, and crouch below his grasp, slicing a line through his gut. The smell is thick and sour as his innards spill out, sloshing to the ground as he falls. I gag, and bile rises in my throat. My eyes water immediately, and it's all I can do not to collapse to my knees.

I'm so busy trying to get myself together that I don't see the third man coming. Before I can think to fight him off, two strong arms coil around me as my mother continues to scream. He squeezes, and I can't breathe. The knife falls from my hand as I thrash wildly. He's yelling at me in his foreign tongue, but I can't even draw breath to tell him that I don't understand. Just as my vision begins to explode with light, I manage to kick the side of the carriage hard enough to topple us both into the new-fallen snow. He falls flat to his back, and I crash on top of him. I hear the air violently rush form his lungs, and he releases me. Rolling to my feet, I scoop up the knife and run as fast as my numb feet will carry me.

The woods are thick and blanketed with snow. I'm light enough that I don't sink too deep as I fly through the forest, but behind me, I hear the crunch of the snow as my attacker pursues, each step slow and labored.

Good. Let him chase me. I can get him away from my mother, then, hopefully, double back and grab her. We will unhitch the sled, and she and I can ride on to St. Petersburg with just the horses. The sky is grey and the air frigid in my lungs. Each breath burns, and then expels in a ball of steam out of my mouth. Still, I run. Turning to spare a glance over my shoulder unbalances me and I fall, slipping down the slope of a hill, tumbling into a deep snow bank. I lay there for a moment, trying to catch my breath and staring at the sky above me, and I listen for his footsteps.

There's nothing.

Rolling onto my side, I peek up. The snow is deep, well over my knees, and I struggle to get back to solid ground. A patch of pine trees offers respite. The snow around them is shallow, and I take a minute to brush the ice from my hair. It has fallen free from its elegant braid and dangles in wet clumps around my face. Still, I have somehow managed to hold onto the knife.

In the distance, I hear a gun shot. The sound echoes through the bleak forest like cannon fire. I turn without hesitation and run back toward my mother, cursing my stupidity. What had I been thinking leaving her alone like that? The bandit must have doubled back to her, thinking me long gone. As I make my way up the steep hill, I slip and fall to my knees in something slimy and wet. It isn't snow but mud, a small spring of warm water bubbling up from the ground. Somehow, the snow had hidden it from my sight, but now, it's all down the front of me. The water and mud pulls down on my already-ruined gown, as if trying to hold me to the earth. I frown at the sight. Poor Mother. She'd paid the seamstress what little money we had to refashion this dress for me. It had been one of her old walking gowns but the seamstress had added lace and a beautiful yellow sash, all of which was now covered in muck. With haste, I untie the sash and slip the bulky gown over my head. The chill is immediate, but still, I feel lighter, light enough to run once more. I run my hands over my corset and decide to rid myself of it while I'm at it. Using the knife, I quickly cut the strings and discard it. Not only can I take a real breath, but also my petticoat is clean and white as snow, helping me blend in. Scrambling back to my feet, I press forward. As soon as I appear over the ridge, I see a man standing at the edge of the cliff not five feet to my left. He looks over, his eyes locking with mine.

He doesn't look like a bandit, I realize. He wears a long, black brocade jacket with golden embroidery; a black, fur hat stuffed on his head makes his blue eyes glow like azure. He's clean, calm, and holding a rife—which is pointed at me for only a moment before he lowers it, a confused expression on his face. I hold out my tiny blade in front of me, as if it would do any good. He cocks his head to the side curiously before addressing me in perfect German.

"Princess Sophia? I'm Sergei Salkov of Her Majesty's Imperial Court. I'm here to rescue you."

Just as the words leave his mouth, something moves in the corner of my eye. The bandit who has been chasing me rushes forward from behind a thick tree, right toward Sergei. The tall, scruffy man is draped in heavy furs and even at full speed, he's moving too slowly to cross the distance between them before I turn the knife in my hand and throw it. It lands with a dull thud in the center of his chest. He swears loudly and then falls forward, the snow around him turning to crimson slush.

As gently as possible, I wrap my arms around my waist and hug myself, rubbing the exposed skin to stave off the frigid cold. I glance up and see Sergei has his rifle lowered at the ground and is staring at the now-fallen bandit. Then he's looks back at me with his mouth twisted into a funny grin.

Not sure what the protocol is for meeting a stranger in my undergarments, I dip into a formal curtsy. "It is a pleasure to meet you, sir, but I think perhaps you are a bit late for that."

Chapter Two

The sound my mother makes when I step back into sight near the road is somewhere between relief and exasperation. Beside her, two royal guards are trying to reload the toppled trunks of gowns, but she turns and orders them to stop. I look over and see that each dress, so carefully refitted and repurposed, has been shredded. Surely, the bandits didn't do such a thing?

"Leave them. They have been utterly destroyed." She turns to me, wearing an expression of shock and indignation, "Can you imagine? Bandits? What a dreadful thing. Thank heavens Her Majesty thought to send us a royal escort or we would both be dead!"

Her face flushes as her voice raises pitch. No doubt, she is thinking even now how this tragedy might be used to her advantage. Her head snaps back to me, as if she's really looking at me for the first time.

"My heavens, Sophie! Where are your clothes? Did that horrible man…?" She doesn't finish the sentence. I know where her mind is spinning off to. If he had touched me in any way, I would be ruined. Sullied and unfit to marry the prince.

"No, Mother. I only fell in some thick mud. I had to rid myself of the gown in order to escape."

She lowers her chin and appraises me carefully, as if she could see the damaged virtue like a spot on her favorite table linen. Finally, she nods, accepting me at my word. Beside me, Sergei slips off his coat and drapes it over my shoulders. It's warm and soft and smells vaguely like the winter pine of my homeland.

"Here you go, Princess. You must have a terrible chill. Would you like us to make a fire for you to warm yourself before we continue to the palace?"

His voice is tender, the way a person might speak to a child. I'm not sure why, but it unsettles me. Perhaps it is pride, but I don't like it at all.

"I'm quite all right, I assure you. I think my mother would be quite pleased to ride on ahead. No need to make a fuss." I pause. "And please, call me Sophie."

He bows his head. "As you wish, Sophie."

He barks orders to his men, who form a tight ring around the carriage with their horses.

"Are you quite certain those bandits won't come back?" Mother asks as she hikes up her skirts and climbs back into the sled.

Sergei smiles, winking at me behind her back. I catch his eye, and a small warmth forms in my belly.

"I'm quite sure they are gone. And should we be set upon again, I'm sure young Sophie will defend your honor."

I can't help but grin at his words. I carefully climb in behind Mother, and Sergei follows me.

"In any case, I shall ride here with you—for your protection, of course."

Mother shrugs indifferently, and Sergei takes a seat beside me.

"They destroyed all our lovely gowns," Mother begins, not meeting his eyes. "We will need new ones. And since this attack occurred on Her Majesty's road—"

Sergei waves her off as if it's nothing. "Yes, of course. I will let the empress know the situation. I'm sure she will make recompense."

Mother nods and sits back, closing her eyes as the carriage rolls into motion.

Sergei leans over to me, his voice a whisper.

"Where did you learn to handle a knife like that?"

Mother answers, her eyes still closed, but her nose wrinkling up in disgust as she speaks.

"Her father let the child run quite wild during our time in Settin. Too indulgent, I always told him so. Young ladies should be taught to sing and sew, not to fight and swing a sword. Still, dangerous times he would say. Posh. To this day, the girl can't sew a straight line and her singing voice is just awful." As if suddenly aware she was articulating all the wrong things to a man who, for all she knew, had the ear of the empress, she sits up starkly, opening her eyes. "That is, Princess

Sophia's strength lies in other accomplishments. She can play the piano quite well, she can read Latin, and she is in every way a true Lady of Prussia."

"I quite agree," Sergei says gently. Mother nods and rests back again. Within minutes, she's snoring gently.

Even under the warmth of his coat, I'm shivering. I hope Sergei doesn't notice the uncontrollable shaking as we bounce along. After a few minutes, he takes my hands in his. I open my mouth to protest, but he brings my fingers to his mouth and blows on them. The warmth of his breath feels so good against my frozen skin that I almost sigh in relief. He repeats the process a few times, blowing my hands and then rubbing them with his. All the while, I'm watching his face. It's not a romantic gesture, yet it's strangely intimate. I don't think I've ever been touched like this before, not by a man—and a terribly handsome man at that. My heart races in my chest, making me warm with flush.

"Better?" he asks finally.

I nod, taking my hands back reluctantly and folding them in my lap. "Yes. Thank you."

He grins. "So, tell me about yourself, Princess."

The muscles in my back stiffen. I wait for a moment, half expecting my mother to jump in with some nonsense about my feminine skills, most of which are blatantly untrue.

"I like to ride," I say weakly.

"Do you hunt?" he asks.

I nod. "I'm a good shot too."

A strange lump forms in my throat, as I realize I may never hunt with my father again.

"Good," Sergei says cryptically, peeking his head out of the carriage window.

"Does that happen often? The attack, I mean. Do you often have a problem with bandits on the road?"

He sits back, looking at me thoughtfully before answering.

"No, never."

"Then why did the empress send you to escort us?" I ask.

He's quiet, looking lost in thought. "The empress didn't send me."

I watch as an array of emotions play out across his chiseled face, worry, dread, and finally, resignation. He says nothing else, but I can read the tension in his squared shoulders, the tick working in his jaw.

"It wasn't a random attack, was it?" I ask boldly. "It was an assassination attempt."

His eyes flicker to mine. "You are a surprising creature, Princess. Clever as well as brave. Wherever did you come from?"

I ignore the backhanded compliment.

"Why would someone attack us?"

He frowns, wiping his hand down his face and rubbing his neck.

"There are those in court who are unhappy at the

prospect of an alliance between Prussia and Russia, those who seek instead to fortify a bond with Austria. The empress favors you and your family, but that favor will extend only so far. If they can prove you unfit—in any way—she will have no choice but to send you away and find an Austrian princess to put on the throne."

I take a deep breath, drawing myself up in my seat.

"Then I must be sure they have no complaint against me. Thank you for your honesty. I appreciate your warnings, and I will heed them." I pause before adding, "And thank you for riding out to save us."

Reaching up, he picks a small clump of mud from my hair.

"Oh, I suspect you had the situation well in hand."

I drift in and out of sleep as we ride on through the day. Just as dusk falls, Sergei nudges me gently.

"We have arrived, Princess."

Pushing back the curtain, I watch out the window as we roll into the grand city of St. Petersburg. Even in the dim glow of the setting sun, the view is breathtaking. The iron-and-gold gates of the Winter Palace stretch before us, the Romanov crest, a glorious golden crowned eagle, watching us from the top. The carriage stops and Sergei steps out, speaking to the guards in quick Russian. The gates slide open and we roll inside, Sergei waving to me as we pass. The grounds are a menagerie of ice sculptures and glowing lanterns. I expect the carriage to stop in front of the grand entrance but it continues, rounding to the rear of the massive estate. Two guards step forward to assist us out as Sergei reappears and leads us into the servants' entrance.

"Why on earth were we not greeted formally?" Mother demands as we weave through the empty kitchens. The hearth is roaring with fire, and I can feel the chill melting out of my skin.

"Surely you would not have the young princess introduced to court in just her petticoats?" Sergei says in the tone one might use with a whining child.

She sighs. "No, of course not."

He tilts his head in a gesture of deference and leads on, up the back staircase and down the left wing of a long, ornate hallway. The walls are marble and granite with decorative, golden wreaths and swirling vines along the ceiling. Massive frescos and beautifully woven tapestries hang from the walls, while tables with fresh-cut flowers sit at every door. I'm tempted to remark on the absurdity of it—fresh flowers in the middle of winter. Being raised by a man who saw such things as unnecessary frivolities, it's an instant reaction. But I'm sure here, at the Grand Imperial Court, they don't have an old man hunched over a ledger complaining about the cost of tulips, so

I bite my tongue. I must remember that here, excess is completely ordinary and I ought not to make a fuss about it.

"These are your rooms," he says motioning to the last door at the end of the hall. The steward pushes the massive, oak door open, and the sitting room inside is nearly the size of my entire home back in Settin. There's a writing desk, piano, and half a dozen chairs and chaises scattered about. A large, round table boasts a silver tray full of meats, cheeses, and breads. There are three doors beyond, two seem to be bedchambers, but I'm not sure about the third. I'm quite sure these rooms alone are the size of our entire home back in Germany. I look to Mother, who frowns, unimpressed.

"Are the accommodations to your liking?" Sergei asks me directly, as Mother begins touring the room, commenting on the color of the drapes and the size of the fireplace.

I nod. "They are; thank you."

"Then I will leave you to rest. I will send up a maid with some nightclothes, and I will have the seamstress attend you first thing in the morning."

Mother turns, "Do tell the empress we've arrived. I'm sure she will be most excited to see me."

Sergei bows gallantly. His eyes flicker up for only a moment and catch mine. A sly grin spreads across his face as he stands and turns to leave, the white-wigged steward closing the door behind them. No sooner are they gone than Mother opens the third door and nods happily.

"A washroom. Good. I could use a hot bath after such a strenuous journey." She turns to look at me. I hold up the hem of my soiled petticoat. She frowns. "You will need to wash too, of course. But I should go first. You will spoil the water with your muck."

Opening our door, she orders the steward back, demanding hot water be brought up from the kitchens.

Sometime later, the water has grown cool as I finally slip out of my clothes and into the tub. Still, it's warm on my cold skin. The soap smells like honey and goats milk as I wash away the last of the snow and mud from my body and hair. I rest back against the side of the copper washtub and try to imagine in my head what it might be like to see Peter again. He would have grown devastatingly handsome, that much I can be sure of, and he will see me and smile. He will take my hand, we will dance and laugh, and he will insist we go for a walk in the garden. The moonlight will be pale and glowing, he will look into my eyes, and… I let the vision trail off. For a moment, one insane second, it wasn't Peter, but Sergei's face in my thoughts. I brush it aside quickly. Sergei is a kind man, handsome, and not much older than I am. A gentleman who went out of his way to keep me safe. But even so, he is not the reason I'm here, and I cannot afford to be distracted by a few kind words and handsome eyes.

I must win the heart of the future king.

"Come along, dear. As I expected, we have been summoned to see the empress first thing in the morning. You will need to be rested."

With a heavy sigh, I step out of the bath and dry myself before slipping into the soft, green dressing gown the maid brought for me.

When I walk into the room, Mother is sitting at the writing desk, furiously scribbling notes on parchment.

"Are you writing Father? To let him know we arrived safely?" I ask.

She looks up at me and blinks, as if the idea was so foreign that it never crossed her mind.

"Of course not. I'm writing to King Fredrick."

"Oh," I say flatly.

King Fredrick of Germany had been overjoyed at the prospect of my sitting on the throne when we stopped for a visit in Berlin on our way here. He sees it as a way to secure an alliance, Mother sees it as a way to regain her lifestyle, and I see it as the only alternative to marrying my Uncle Edward.

She points the feather quill at me. "Make no mistake, Sophia, this union is a political alliance sanctioned by the king himself. And if you are successful in securing the prince's hand in marriage, our family will be rewarded with wealth enough to rival the most prestigious noble's in Berlin."

I freeze. The thought of facing this task alone is beyond daunting. Dread shoots up my back like spikes.

"Will you go back then? Back to Prussia?"

She pauses, then sets down the pen and holds her hands out to me. I step forward and take them. "Sweet child. I will never leave you. For as long as you need me by your side, I will remain. Even if it means living with these monstrous Russian winters."

I smile, relief flooding through me. Mother might be shallow and, at times, callous, but what she does, she does for me and for our family. It's easy to forget that sometimes.

She sends me off to bed; the warm blankets and soft pillows soothe me into an instant slumber. All too soon, I see the first rays of daylight sneaking through the slit in the curtains. The maid from last night rushes in and throws them open, flooding the room with warmth and light. I sit up, rubbing my eyes.

"Thank you," I mutter. "I'm sorry; I've forgotten your name."

The maid curtsies. "Isobel, my lady."

"Thank you, Isobel. Is the seamstress here yet?"

"She only just arrived."

"Thank you," I say, throwing back the blankets. Isobel gathers them and begins making the bed as I step out into the foyer.

There are three trunks of gowns, all open and overflowing as Mother and the seamstress bicker. As soon as I enter, the seamstress bows her neck.

"My lady."

I nod. "What is all this?"

"Fifteen gowns," Mother says, throwing her hands in the air dramatically. "You are getting fifteen new gowns."

I step forward. "That's wonderful."

Mother snorts in disagreement. "No, it's barely enough to replace what we lost. And I am only getting nine."

I don't remind her that we only had four gowns between us, and that they were mysteriously destroyed. Or that all four were old and had been remade at least half a dozen times already.

Instead, I turn to the seamstress. "The empress is too generous. We are grateful."

The seamstress smiles and motions for me to come to her. She appraises me thoughtfully.

"You are about the size of my daughter, lucky enough. She often stands for me to try new fabrics and styles on. And your coloring, the brown hair and dark blue eyes, you will look lovely in most colors. I'm so glad. Only last week we had to work for a lady with hair orange as fire and pale skin. There were so few colors we could put her in that didn't make her look sick."

She prattles on under the watchful eye of my mother as she discusses patterns, bustle sizes, and sashes. I just close my eyes, lift my arms when told to, and let them choose. There's a sharp tap at the door and the steward comes in, a large box in his arms. He sets it on the floor and backs up.

"A gift from Lord Salkov."

Mother shoos the steward out and opens the box, pulling out a lovely pink-and-black lace gown. The style is French, a low bodice and tight sleeves. Compared to anything else I've ever had, it's downright scandalous. Yet, I remember seeing many ladies dressed in similar styles in Berlin and the idea of wearing it, looking so grown up, makes my heart pound. The notion of Sergei admiring me in it makes my heart pound harder.

Mother holds it up to herself and grins wildly. "It's just lovely. I think I'll go put it on."

"Don't be silly. It's for the princess. See the cut of the waist? It's far too narrow for you," the seamstress says, not looking up from her work.

Frowning, Mother drapes the gown over her arm. "Insolent girl. The gown is obviously for me."

I shrug, "Maybe he's put a note in the box?"

Mother walks to the box and pulls a tiny scrap of paper out, reading it aloud.

"'Since you have no gown to wear today, please accept this humble gift.' It's signed Sergei Salkov. It doesn't say who it's for."

I point to her bedchamber. "You have the gown you were wearing yesterday. I have no gown at all," I say simply.

She glares at me. "I can't wear that. It's filthy."

The seamstress looks up at me with sympathy in her eyes.

"Well, then I suppose I will have to meet the empress naked. I'm sure she will understand, Mother. I mean, it wouldn't make her think less of me—of my fitness to marry her nephew—to meet her like this, don't you think? Yes, I'm sure she will understand."

I hold my breath. I've never employed this particular tactic with her before, and I'm not sure how she will react. I've put her vanity against her plotting as I've seen my father do so many times. It's always a risk. Sometimes, she would react with a quiet acceptance of his will. Other times, she simply tightened her mouth into a line and left, scheming behind his back until she achieved her goals.

She stares at me for a second before tossing the gown on the seat beside me.

"You are quite right, of course. A kind gift though it is, I will simply have to let you borrow it for the day. I'm sure Sergei will understand."

And with that, she spins on her heel and heads into her bedchamber, closing the door behind her. On her knees in front of me, the seamstress smiles widely and winks at me.

The maid is helping me into my gown when the steward arrives with a request from the empress to join her for breakfast in her private chambers. Mother, dressed and leaving her room for the first time since her tantrum, accepts the invitation graciously and helps Isobel finish buttoning the dress. Behind me, Mother drapes something across my neck. Catching a glimpse of it in the mirror as she fastens the clasp, I gasp softly. It's one of the few jewels her family passed down to her, and one of her prized possessions. A dozen black-onyx teardrops dangle from a strand of black beads at the base of my neck. The stones are warm against my skin and I wonder if she's been holding them all this time, debating whether to put them on me or wear them herself. Apparently, her desire to put me on the throne is greater than her own vanity—which is something I won't soon forget.

After all, Johanna of Holsein-Gottorp was born a princess, the great-granddaughter of the King of Denmark, but after being forced to marry a man beneath her rank, she lost nearly everything. The jewels were all she had, the last link to the bright future that had—in her mind—been stolen from her. Now, with an opportunity to set me on a throne, she hopes to reclaim a little bit of that future. I'm not about to complain. Not when, until the empress' invitation arrived, she had been content to marry me off to the highest bidder, no matter how wretched the prospects might be.

And I have no doubt that if I fail in this endeavor, that is exactly the fate that I will return home to.

With that in mind, I straighten myself up, smooth my bustle, and raise my chin. Mother twists my hair into a lovely, but simple roll across my forehead and secures it with a pin. Finally ready, we follow the steward out of the room ant toward the empress' chambers.

Chapter Three

The empress is surrounded by her ladies when we arrive. They are all seated around a large, mahogany table covered in food and even from her chair, I can tell she's a head taller than the women around her are. She has wide, brilliant blue eyes, a full, rosy mouth, and a soft, round face. Her blonde hair is powdered not the usual white, but coal black. She takes a bite of candied pear, and my stomach turns. I realize for the first time that I haven't eaten since the day before, and I've grown ravenous. As soon as we enter, Mother and I curtsy gracefully.

"Your Majesty," we say in unison.

"Ah yes. Thank you for joining us," she says graciously, motioning with a wave of her hand for us to take a seat. Out the corner of my eye, I see Sergei and two other men I don't know standing in the far corner of the room. He washes a glance over me with a pleased expression, and it sends chills across my flesh. With a clap of her hands, Empress Elizabeth dismisses her ladies. I watch as the movement ruffles the large, black feather that stands upright in her hair, draping across her head and curving down the other side, caressing her pale cheek.

"I was so sorry to hear of that nasty business in on the road. I trust you are both well and unharmed?"

She glances from Mother to me, and Mother answers.

"We are quite well, Your Majesty. Though our belongings were mostly destroyed."

"Yes, Sergei has informed me," the empress says dryly.

I speak softly, "Thank you, Your Majesty, for being so kind as to replace our gowns."

That earns me a slight smile as she pokes a bit of cheese with a fork and stuffs it into her mouth.

"Yes, you are too kind," Mother adds after a moment of silence.

The empress stares at me appraisingly. Her dress is silver, trimmed with gold lace, and almost every inch of her exposed skin is covered in diamonds. Her vestige is overwhelming. It's all I can do to meet her gaze and not look away.

"Sergei tells me you fought off the bandits single-handedly?" she asks, a wry smile turning up the edges of her lips.

Beside me, I feel Mother stiffen.

"I'm sure it had more to do with the timely arrival of your guards," Mother offers modestly.

The empress ignores her. "Sergei tells me you

fought them off with a knife? Is that true?"

I nod. "Yes, Your Majesty."

"That is quite—"

My mother cuts her off. "Unbecoming a lady, and I've told her as much. But have no worries, Your Majesty, I'm sure it was a solitary occurrence. The instinct for a child to protect their mother is a strong thing."

The empress shoots her a withered look before turning back to me.

"I was going to say courageous. Don't you agree, Chancellor Bestuzhev?" she asks. A dark-haired man steps forward from behind Sergei. He's wearing a simple grey tunic, breeches with a black jacket, and a belt of gold-encrusted rubies drapes from his shoulders. It looks very similar to the blood-red stones in the empress' tiara, a matching set of royal jewels.

He bows from the neck. "Quite courageous, Your Majesty."

For the first time, I watch as the empress' face softens and she smiles genuinely, sitting back and gently wiping her mouth with her linen napkin.

"And what do you have to say, Count Lestocq?"

The third man steps forward. He's short and rotund but somehow still handsome, with flushed cheeks and warm, amber-colored eyes.

"I would say that Your Majesty has chosen well. It will take a brave wife indeed to stand next to Peter."

His words seem to be a compliment, but there's

an underlying tone that bothers me. A feeling that the words were carefully chosen to have a secondary meaning that I do not understand.

"Yes. But of course, the decision hasn't been made yet, Count," Bestuzhev says curtly. "There are still many variables. The treaty for one thing—"

The empress sighs heavily and waves her hand, effectively silencing him.

"Yes, yes. The treaty. I am well aware. But I tire of politics. I want to know more about our young princess. Tell me, Sophie, what do you think of Russia so far?"

Her tone is light, but there is a weight to her words.

"Russia is beautiful, Your Majesty. I cannot wait to see it in the spring bloom. I'm sure it's splendid to behold."

She grins. "And do you speak Russian?"

I shake my head just a fraction. "Sadly, no. I speak German and French, and I can read and write in Latin as well. Though I hope to take up the study of the language while I'm here. My mother was just mentioning during our journey that my education would not be complete until I've mastered it."

Beside me, Mother sits up a little taller, a modest grin gracing her lovely face.

"Well, it's settled then. General Salkov can be your tutor. Beyond helping you master our beautiful language, he can also teach you the customs of court and see to your safety during your visit."

At the word *visit*, Mother visibly tenses.

Just then, the door to her chamber sweeps open and Peter bounds into the room as if on horseback. Seeing me, he grins wildly, his blue eyes dancing mischievously, just as they did when he was a little boy. But his face is longer and more defined, a hint of stubble rides his jaw, and he's gotten tall, taller than even Sergei. He bows quickly to his aunt, then to my mother, before crossing the room in two long strides and taking me by the waist, lifting me into the air, and twirling me gently before sitting me back on my feet.

"Sophie how glorious it is to see you again."

He turns back to the empress. "I'm sorry, dear Aunt, but I could wait no longer."

She smiles warmly and waves him off.

"How have you been? How is Prussia?" he asks quickly, ignoring my mother's uncomfortable cough.

"Very well to both," I say, unable to keep the smile from my face. "And you?"

He shrugs. "As well as can be expected in such deplorable conditions." He shoots a grin over his shoulder to his aunt, who is watching us with a wistful look on her face. "I've had no one to play Whist with."

I can't suppress the laugh that follows his words.

"That's probably because you cheat so badly."

"I cheat quite well, thank you," he says, combing back his golden hair with his fingers, then letting it fall back into a mound of curls.

The empress stands, and we all turn to face her.

"Tonight, there is a ball in honor of Peter's sixteenth birthday tomorrow. I do hope you will both join us. I would be honored to introduce you to my court," The empress offers gracefully, brushing the breadcrumbs from her bodice.

I curtsy.

"Of course, Your Majesty. We would love to attend," Mother answers for me.

The empress turns her full attention to Mother for the first time.

"Johanna, I must admit, I was so devastated when your dear brother died before we could be wed. I have always felt that destiny was somehow subverted when our houses were not joined in marriage."

Mother inclines her head. "I have felt that as well, Your Majesty. But I believe that destiny, and anything that is truly meant to be, will always find a way to right itself."

Peter faces me and, bowing, takes my hand in his, bringing it gently to his lips.

"I look forward to it," he offers with a depth in his voice, and I can't help but wonder if he means seeing me at the ball… or something else entirely.

The empress steps forward, taking Peter's arm, and they exit together, leaving Mother and me to return to our chambers. Within moments of returning, Sergei and Count Lestocq arrive, followed by a flurry of attendants and footmen. They bow graciously, both men looking pleased with us.

"Ladies, let me be the first to congratulate you. You have made a splendid impression with Her Majesty. She is quite taken with young Sophie," the count offers with a grin, handing my mother a large, leather satchel.

Mother huffs, opening the sack, "Of course she is. My daughter is a rare jewel. One would have to be blind not to see her beauty and grace..." Her voice trails off as a handful of gold and silver rubles falls out into her hand. She gawks only for a moment before gathering herself, slipping the money back in the purse and looking back up at Sergei. "My daughter is worth much more than the contents of this purse."

I blush at her words. More than once growing up, Mother had openly complained about how plain and boyish I was. To hear her speak of me so warms my heart.

"I quite agree," the count says firmly, holding his arm out to my mother. "And I see where her beauty and grace have come from. Let me assure you, that is only the beginning of Her Majesty's grace. Much more will follow. But for now, may I interest you in a tour of the palace, my lady?"

Her eyes light up, and then flicker hesitantly in my direction.

He continues. "Sergei is eager to begin her Russian lessons and the servants will be busy for hours preparing your gowns for this evening, far too tedious for a lady such as yourself to be forced to endure, don't you agree?"

At his words, she tucks her chin bashfully and accepts his arm.

"You are quite right, of course. A tour would be delightful."

As soon as they are gone, I feel the air around me thicken. Sergei is watching me with his hypnotic blue eyes and despite the other people in the room, I feel quite alone under his gaze, as if we were the only people in existence.

Finally, he raises one eyebrow. "Sophie, you are a clever girl, tell me, did you pick up on anything during your audience with the empress?"

I take a seat in the red velvet chair near the window overlooking the river.

"Well, it's quite obvious that Chancellor Bestuzhev isn't pleased with my arrival."

He nods silently.

"He seems quite taken with Austria and his treaty," I add thoughtfully. "Do you think he was behind the attack on my carriage?"

Sergei sits down, leaning forward with his elbows on his knees. "You will find there are many people here at court that fears the Prussian influence. Peter himself is so taken with King Fredrick that it's practically all he talks about. There are those who worry that under Peter's rule, Russia would become nothing more than a puppet to the demands of Prussia."

I lower my chin, looking him in the eye.

"That wasn't an answer to my question."

He shrugs. "I have no answer to give. It's possible, yes. I would not put it past him, but there are others as well who could have had a hand in it. I simply do not know."

"So even here, at the palace, I'm no safer than I was in those woods. There are still powerful people who wish me gone."

"That is true, but I did share my concerns for your safety with the empress. That is partly why she named me your tutor. I'm also your unofficial guard."

I almost quip that being under his guard doesn't make me feel any better, but I hold back the words because deep down, I do actually feel safer knowing he's watching over me.

"And," I continue as gently as possible, "it was so nice to see Peter again. Though the count's remarks surprised me. Tell me, what kind of a man is Peter?"

For the first time, Sergei shifts in his chair, looking a bit uncomfortable.

"Peter is… young. He has a great love of all things German and military. He speaks German only, so you must always address him in such, and he can be extremely short-tempered."

I grin. "So he's much unchanged then."

Sergei smiles sadly. "Lestocq is right about one thing; it will take a very clever, very strong woman to rein him in. The empress knows as much. She's not just looking for a wife for him—she's looking for someone formidable enough to tame him."

I take a deep breath, not daring to speak the words floating in my mind. I cannot admit, even to myself, how desperately I hope for him to fall madly in love with me. For years, I watched my parents suffer in their arranged marriage, barely tolerating each other. Is it so wrong to dream of romance and tenderness? Of love?

"And that's not all. There are two other ladies arriving today, Lady Elizavetta and Lady Ekaterina Vorontsova. Neither is a princess, but they are from one of the wealthiest, most influential families in Russia. They've been asked to serve as your ladies-in-waiting while you're here, but make no mistake, if you are found unsuitable for marriage to Peter, they will be in line behind you—and either of them is a much more suitable match for him in the eyes of the anti-Prussian movement at court."

I nod, unable to keep the frown from my face.

Reaching out, Sergei lays a hand on mine. My shivers from earlier return and I gaze at him.

"This task will not be an easy one. The road to your coronation will be long, and fraught with danger and treachery. Are you certain this is what you want?" His expression is soft and full of kindness. If I choose to leave, I need only say so now, and he will see me safely home, back to the house of my father. For a moment, the idea fills me with joy. Then I remember that my joy would be short-lived. Two seasons from now, we will be so in debt that we will be forced to sell off our lands, and our kingdom and title will be taken. Mother, Father, and my sweet baby brother will live in poverty for the rest of their days and I, well, I will be sent off to marry my uncle. A slow chill crawls up my spine, and I have to fight off a shudder.

"My choice, General Salkov, is to do whatever necessary to win Peter's heart and the crown that accompanies it," I say boldly.

He sits back.

"Then I am at your service, Princess Sophie. But know this—it's not Peter's heart you should be concerned with. You must win the heart of the empire."

I nod, squaring my shoulders and tilting my chin upward.

"Then perhaps we should begin with my first lesson." I take a piece of paper from the desk and scribble on it. "Tell me, how do you say this in Russian?" I ask, sliding him the paper.

He grins.

Chapter Four

As Sergei predicted, the Ladies Vorotsova arrive at midday in a golden carriage. Their entourage is small, and they have a brief audience with both Empress Elizabeth and Count Lestocq before being sent to my rooms. By the time they arrive, I have three new gowns completed and my mother has returned from her long walk, a radiant smile plastered across her face. The girls greet me with deep curtsies. Elizavetta is short and plump with orange red hair and round eyes so light blue that they remind me of the morning sky. She's round in the face and shoulders like the paintings of angelic cherubs, only her plump lips are dark red with beet juice, taking her look from childish to voluptuous. Her sister is nearly the exact opposite. Ekaterina has golden yellow hair that hangs in long, loose waves down her back. She is slender but not sharp of feature, her smile rich and genuine. Only her eyes betrayed their relation, the same light, icy blue.

"I'm so pleased to meet you," I offer warmly. "I

hope your journey was pleasant."

Ekaterina speaks first. "It was quite uneventful. And please, call me Rina."

I nod. Elizavetta steps forward, looking flushed.

"Is there anything you need right now, my lady? I should like to see to our things."

I shake my head. "I'm all right for now. Please, see to your things and settle in. In a few hours, I will need your help preparing for tonight's ball."

With a curt nod, the red-haired sister glides off to her own room next door. Rina, however, stays behind. Mother quietly excuses herself, grabs the paper and ink well, and heads to her private chambers, closing the door behind her.

Soon, I hear yelling from the next room, Elizavetta screaming at the servants about mishandling their trunks. I turn a surprised glance to Rina, who blushes wildly.

"I think you will find my dear sister is… unused to serving others, as she is much more accustomed to being served." She bats her eyelashes. "I blame my father really. He has spoiled her to the point of making her an incurable brat."

I can't help but laugh at the remark, because it reminds me of something very similar I said about my own brother once. At the memory, a sharp pain erupts behind my ribs, a longing for home that always seems to be just below the surface.

"I will leave her to the unpacking, I think.

Retribution for the many, many verses of poetry she felt the need to recite on the journey." She grins at me conspiratorially. "How are you settling into court? It must be very different than where you're from."

I'm not sure whether I should be offended by the remark, so I choose to wave it off.

"It's very similar, on a larger scale, of course."

She kneels down and begins gathering up discarded bits of fabric and lace.

"Are you hungry?" I ask suddenly. She looks up, a bit startled.

"I am famished."

I turn to the maid. "Isobel, could you fetch some food for me and my lady? Some salted meat and bread with honey, please."

With a quick curtsy, Isobel hurries off to the kitchen.

"Please, sit with me, Rina."

She obliges, sitting in a chair across from me.

"Tell me, Rina, have you ever been to one of the empress' balls?"

She nods. "Quite often. My family visits court regularly."

"So you must know the prince?"

She frowns. "I have seen him a few times, but we've never spoken. He rarely attends the galas and when he does, he's always surrounded by his men."

"His men?"

"Young generals and advisors he keeps close to

him. Alexander Mananov and Mikhail Andrei, most specifically. They are his closest companions."

I nod, repeating the names in my mind until I've memorized them.

"Surely, he will be there this evening. It's in his honor after all," I offer pleasantly.

She shrugs. "I'm sure you're right. He will be there, if only on orders from his aunt."

She turns her head to the side, looking at me thoughtfully.

"Have you never met him then? The prince, that is."

"Once, a long time ago. Honestly, I was afraid he wouldn't even remember me, but when I saw him earlier…" I let myself trail off. I can still feel where his hands clasped my waist; his smile has brined itself into my memory. I feel myself blush at the thought.

She smiles warmly. "Then we have our work cut out for us. After tonight, Princess, everyone in court will know your name."

Isobel is just beginning to light the lamps in my chambers when Rina is finished. She and my mother have managed to twist my hair into an elaborate design with curls and ribbons piled high on my head. I'm wearing a gown of soft sky blue with a large pannier bustle that makes the fabric wide over my hips. The top is cut low, swung across my upper arms to expose my neck and shoulders, only the soft organza in the bodice keeping my breasts from spilling out. Rina laces a pearl choker around my neck and completes the transformation with a small, pearl tiara from her own trunk.

"It's so lovely," I say softly.

She shrugs, as if it means less than nothing.

"There. You are all done. I will go slip into my gown, and I'll be back in a few minutes to escort you to the staircase."

As she slips out the door, Elizavetta comes back in. If my dress is large, hers is simply massive. Dark crimson satin, her gown is cut the same as mine in the bodice. Only without the grace of the organza, her ample bosom is on full display like a trussed ham on a platter. The red is the same color as her lips and the large, ruby tiara in her hair. The color, while bold, makes her skin look a bit green and unsettled, and it draws the natural flush from her round cheeks.

She curtsies. "My lady."

I nod and turn back to the mirror, examining myself carefully one last time. My mother slips a dark blue sash over my head, and I secure it across my chest. She turns to Elizavetta and puts her hand to her chest in shock.

"Oh my. What a bold gown, wherever did you get it?"

The girl smiles.

“Paris, my lady. A gift from my uncle, the Imperial Chancellor.”

“Paris,” Mother mumbles. “That certainly explains it.”

Rina returns, her hair coiled into a wispy braid and fastened to the crown on her head. Her gown is the colors of spun gold, making her look like a radiant sun. She’s put a little coal along her eyes, and it makes them stand out against her otherwise porcelain skin.

Mother steps in front of them.

“Now, when we are introduced, I will lead my daughter down the grand staircase. You two will follow behind.”

They both nod. Mother opens the door and announces to the steward, “We are ready.”

He leads us down the hallway and through the corridor in the main part of the palace. Every room we pass is rich with color and finery. We go down two flights of stairs and end up on the west side of the staircase. Sergei is there waiting, along with Count Lestocq, who immediately takes Mother’s arm. Holding his arm out for me, Sergei smiles.

“May I have the honor?”

He’s traded his earlier attire for a navy-blue velvet Caftan with gold embroidery. The color is so rich and lush it’s all I can do not to reach out and stroke his arm. Carefully laying my hand atop of his, we line up. Across the staircase from us is Empress Elizabeth on the arm of Chancellor Bestuzhev, her silver gown shining in the lamplight. Behind her, a group of young men laughs good-naturedly.

I pick out Peter immediately.

He turns and our eyes connect for only a heartbeat before the empress steps forward, obscuring him from my sight. Still, I manage to hold that moment in my mind, that perfect moment when he sees me and smiles, his nose and eyes crinkling the way they did when we were little. I can see the very top of his sandy blond curls over her head. A deep sigh slides from my chest at the sight of him. Below us, the music stops and those who were dancing slide to the edges of the room as the valet announces the empress. She glides down the massive marble-and-gold staircase and the entire room honors her, their heads bowed reverently until she walks past.

But I'm not looking at the empress, radiant though she is in her finery. My eyes have locked on Peter's face. He's not looking at me now, but talking with the two young men flanking him. He says something and they laugh heartily, his gaze finally wandering up to mine in an expression I can't quite place. He looks me over and it's all I can do not to fidget under his scrutiny. When his eyes meet mine, again he gently dips his head to me and under my tight bodice, my heart races.

He is announced next, followed by his companions. Then Mother's name is called, and she and the Count begin their descent. Beside me, Sergei pats my arm reassuringly as my name is called. I'm barely aware of my movement until we are nearly halfway down the staircase and I see all eyes on me, some joyful, some apprehensive, and some downright cold. Trumpets blast behind me, and we stop there on the stairs. Empress Elizabeth stands at the base, motioning to us as she makes the announcement.

"Princess Johanna and Princess Sophie have come a very long way to join us tonight. They have, in very short order, proven to be clever, courageous, and strong of faith. For this reason, I would like to bestow a great honor upon them."

With a wave, she motions for us to join her. Sergei releases me and we descend the stairs, neither quite sure what's about to happen.

One of her men steps forward as the guards around the room begin to drum softly. He kneels, holding up a red-velvet pillow on which two sashes and pins sit. Taking one pair, she approaches my mother.

"Princess Johanna, by the authority invested of me by God and man as Empress and the Great and Holy Saint Catherine of Alexandria, I bestow upon you, the Order of Saint Catherine, and the Lesser Star of Russia." She drapes the sash over Mother's head, and then pins the diamond inlaid cross to her bodice, placing a hand on her head to seal the ordination. Then she moves to me.

"Princess Sophia, by the authority invested of me by God and man as Empress and the Great and Holy

Saint Catherine of Alexandria, I bestow upon you, the Order of Saint Catherine, and the Greater Star of Russia."

She repeats the gesture, placing on me the sash of scarlet moiré with silver edges embroidered with the inscription: "ZA LYUBOV' I OTECHESTVO". Then she retrieves the pin, a massive, star-shaped pendant of diamonds and rubies attached to a red bow, and affixes it to my bodice.

She turns, addressing the room, and everyone erupts into joyous cheers.

I step forward and clear my throat.

I recite my short speech in nearly perfect Russian. "Thank you, Empress, for your kind welcome. Though I had never before seen the light of a Russian day, I fell in love the moment the sun rose in the sky. Being here to celebrate Grand Duke Peter's birthday is a joy and a gift. I hope it is the first of many such occasions we will share."

The crowd mutters a warm, "Here, here!" And the empress beams at me.

With a clap of her hands, the music begins and I feel a familiar hand at my elbow. I try to look pleasant, a hint of a smile on my face as Sergei takes me around, making introductions to all the emissaries from other courts. I listen to each with genuine interest even as, out of the corner of my eye, I'm searching for my fair-haired prince. The dance ends, and people clap. When the music begins up again, the empress takes the floor with the handsome, young Duke Rohebin, the envoy from Denmark. Soon, others join them. I glance around nervously. I'm sure Sergei can feel my hand shaking in his, but he says nothing. Behind me, my ladies giggle and flirt with the noble men around us. It takes me a moment to realize that the court is populated with a heavy ratio of men to women. My ladies and I, my mother, and the empress, being part of only a small handful of those in attendance.

When I finally catch sight of Peter, he's across the room, walking towards me, a wide grin across his face. He looks incredibly handsome in his military-style green suit, his stride confident and determined. Reaching me, he stops abruptly and bows.

"My Lady Sophia, General Salkov. It's nice to see you again."

I curtsy.

"It's nice to see you again as well, my lord," I offer.

Sergei bows and politely excuses himself.

"Pardon me. I must see to Sir Rudolpho."

Peter motions with his finger, and a maid brings over two tall goblets of wine. Handing one to me, he takes a long drink from his own before making a terrible face.

"French wine," he complains. "It's as bitter as their people and twice as pretentious."

I take a sip. The red wine is smooth on my tongue, and as soon as I've swallowed it, it begins to warm my belly.

"It could be worse," I say in a whisper. "It could be Portuguese."

He laughs, and it's light and musical.

"True. True. Now, I must know—how was your journey? I hear you had a bit of trouble on the road."

His blue eyes sparkle, telling me he already knows the whole story.

"It was long and tiring. And we were attacked by thieves on the road."

He feigns surprise. "How terrible. Your guard was able to dispatch them?"

I take another long drink of wine before answering.

"No. My guard fell, and I was left to defend my mother and myself."

He grins. "You fought off a group of bandits all on your own?"

I lower my chin, looking up at him from under my eyelashes.

"Most grown men would not expect a woman to fight back, certainly not a girl, and most certainly not a noble girl. The element of surprise is a powerful weapon in such a situation."

"Still, it's quite impressive. You must be skilled with a blade."

"I prefer the bow. Perhaps we could go for a hunt sometime. I could impress you with my very unladylike talents."

As soon as the words escape my mouth, I realize how it's sounded and I flush deep crimson. Before I can apologize for my words, his gaze slips behind me.

"And who are your ladies?" he asks pointedly.

I introduce them, and they curtsy in turn.

The music changes, picking up tempo into an Allemande. Reaching past me, Peter holds out his hand.

"Lady Elizavetta, would you care to dance?"

My heart sinks like a stone in my chest as she accepts with a laugh and smile. They make their way to the dance floor as I attempt to recover from the shock. It had been going so well, hadn't it? I frown. He must have been horribly offended by my remark.

My eyes flicker up to find my mother, gawking at me as if I'd done something completely unthinkable. I blink back tears, handing my goblet to Rina, who sets it on the table next to us. I'm completely prepared to excuse myself to my room and wallow in my shame when two young men approach us and bow.

"Ladies, please allow us an introduction. I am Alexander Mananov, and this is my good friend, Sir Mikhail Andrei."

I bow my head, and Rina curtsies.

"I'm pleased to meet you. Please, call me Sophie. This is my lady, Rina."

Now it's Mikhail's turn to flush.

"We've met," he admits meekly, staring at Rina.

Mikhail looks quite startlingly like Peter, the same blue eyes, the same build—even their hair color is similar. Only Mikhail's face is more slender, his nose rounder at the tip, and he does not smile. He looks quite uncomfortable actually.

Compared to the other boys, Alexander is very dark. His hair is raven, and his deep-set eyes are green flecked with gold. His skin is more olive tone, his smile thin but perfectly shaped, like a cupid's bow. As I look over him closely for the first time, I'm quite stricken. He holds himself in a manner that is both formal and somehow relaxed, and his smile is confident while still genuine.

It's Alexander who holds his hand out to me.

"Well, Princess Sophie, may I have this dance?"

I swallow, unsure what to do. To refuse might appear rude, but I also don't want to risk incurring Peter's wrath by showing attention to one of his companions. I glance over at the dance floor and watch Peter clutch Elizavetta by the waist and spin her across the floor. A wave of recklessness overcomes me.

Turning my gaze back to Alexander, I set my hand in his.

"That would be lovely, thank you."

Without hesitation, he smiles and leads me to the floor. Taking my waist with his free hand, we begin to spin. I watch him as we dance, searching for any hint of duplicity in his expression. But there's nothing that betrays him, nothing that suggests he's anything but genuinely enjoying himself, so I relax, allowing myself to do the same.

"Tell me about yourself, Lord Mananov."

He grins. "Alexander, please."

"Alexander then."

"I'm from Sweden originally, though my mother is of Spanish descent. My father is the ruler of a large principality to the north. I have an older brother, Sven, and three little sisters. My family sent me to court as an ambassador five years ago."

"That must be difficult, being so far from home. Do you miss it?" I ask curiously.

"I miss my family, yes. But I have made a home here."

I smile, but say nothing. I don't want to betray my homesickness or my desperate longing to see my father and brother.

As if sensing my hesitation, he continues. "Don't worry, Princess. I'm sure you will come to love it here, as I have. There are many beautiful and wonderful things to see at court."

"Like what?" I ask playfully.

He looks right into my eye and half smiles, "Well, there's you for one."

"Are you flirting with me?" I ask playfully.

"I wouldn't dream of it. Well, maybe I would, but that doesn't make it less true." He holds my gaze for a heartbeat and I can feel a blush roll up my neck and spread across my face.

"And," he continues, "there is a spot in the east tower where, at sunrise just a few times a year, the light shines in, reflecting off the stained glass in the little chapel, and it's like watching the birth of a rainbow."

"That sound lovely," I say earnestly.

"It is. Perhaps I will show you sometime. How long are you staying?"

I shrug, remembering my mother's earlier words. "I don't know, but I think that my feet may never set foot on German soil again."

"Would that be so terrible?

Looking up at him, I think that it might not be. His eyes are glistening in the lamplight and now that I'm looking at him, really looking at him, I realize how devastatingly handsome he is. Not in a cool, sunshine way like Peter, but in a dark, mysterious way. My heart pounds furiously in my chest as I try to catch my breath. The dancing ends and he bows to me as a new tune begins, slow and calm. Without asking, he steps forward and places his hands on my hips, swaying us gently, together and then apart, a slow turn, then my back is pressed against his front and I feel the length of him, firm and strong before we part again. Each movement somehow both brings us together and moves us apart in a slow, torturous ballet.

We continue to dance and as the night grows on, each movement becomes more and more a torment, an ache to touch him that I can't stop. My heart races, my skin warm with flush. Beside me, I hear the shrill laugh of Elizavetta as Peter twirls her forcefully. I realize for the first time that they both seem very, very drunk.

Across from me, Alexander stills, watching the display with a playful shake of his head.

He motions to me, we step off the dance floor for the first time, and I hesitate only a moment, not quite ready to release the tension building between us. If anyone has noticed Peter's behavior, they aren't showing it—quite the contrary. They are moving around him as if he isn't even there, making me wonder just how common this behavior might be.

Turning to me, Alexander lowers his voice.

"You should know it isn't a slight—him not asking you to dance. It's sort of a… game with him."

Peter always did enjoy his games.

I wrinkle my nose, tilting my head to the side, "A game of what kind?"

"He likes to make women jealous, make them fight for his attention."

I frown. "That seems like a cruel, petty thing to do. What does he hope to accomplish with it?"

"He hopes to determine the depths of your interest I him, before admitting his own interest. It allows him to remain in control."

I look up, staring him right in the eyes.

"And what part do you play in these games?"

He holds up his hands. "None, I assure you. I've seen him enough to know what he's doing. But I couldn't bear the thought of you standing here looking so heartbroken."

I jerk my chin up. "If you think his rudeness in any way damaged my heart, then you are mistaken. I am made from much sterner stuff than that. I'm not the sort of girl to flitter at the attention of a man, nor to weep at the callousness of one."

Perhaps, that's not entirely true. I had been frustrated nearly to tears at his slight, when I thought it was my fault. But knowing it was not my poorly turned phrase but his own egotistical games that spawned his behavior, well, that was a different matter entirely.

"If you intend to win Peter, you must beat him at his own game."

I open my mouth to protest, to declare that love should never be a game, but even as I think it, I begin to doubt it's true. How would I know, after all? It's not as if I have any experience in the matter. No matter how many romantic poems you recite, no matter how many glorious tales of love you read, how can you really understand the condition if you've never found yourself in it?

"How, do you advise, do I do that?"

He grins. "I think it must be like a military attack. Strategic and precise. I have never seen a lady not respond to him, whether in love or in rage. Perhaps your best move is indifference. Perhaps you will have to make him come to you."

"By ignoring him?" How ridiculous that sounds.

"Not ignoring him, but by making him desire you, then making yourself aloof." His words are measured, as if he's unsure how I will react to the idea. I feel myself begin to smirk.

I always did love beating Peter at his own games.

As if he's never left, Sergei slides up next to me, holding out his arm.

"A dance, Princess?"

I nod. Any tension I was feeling toward Alexander before evaporates the moment my hand slips into Sergei's. "Of course, General. Thank you for the dance, Alexander, and for your advice. I shall consider it."

Sergei leads me onto the floor. My heart pounds as we dance, and I realize what I'd been feeling before must have been more a combination of wine and exertion than anything else.

"What advice did the young Lord Mananov give you, pray tell?"

I shrug. "He believes Peter's lack of interest in me this evening is a game or a test of some kind. He suggested I respond by not responding."

Sergei considers that for a moment.

"Wise advice, I think. But be careful, Princess. When waging a war of the heart, you must only fight if you are absolutely sure you can win."

At his warning, my eyes slide over to where Peter has abandoned his dancing partner and sits, jacket undone, wine in hand, laughing with his friends. He looks over to me and winks, taking a deep drink. "If it's war he wants, war it shall be," I decide.

Chapter Five

The night rolls on endlessly. I move between chatting and talking politics with Sergei to somehow dancing with Edmund, The Duke of Buckinghamshire, a visitor to the court from England. He's regaling me with tales of his lovely Brittan and his astute and powerful King George, when I see Mikhail pick up a very drunken Peter under the arm and help him out of the room, toward his bedchamber. Alexander follows after, but not before finding me in the crowd with his eyes and giving me a subtle tilt of the head, which I return.

"Perhaps that is the true purpose of me being here, to keep the peace between our countries," he continues, though I'm only half-paying attention. My thoughts are with Peter and the dark-haired boy, whom I can't quite decide whether I can trust or not. "But it leaves me here to continue to negotiate a peace, with Russia at least."

I nod softly. England and France are a hair's breadth from one side or the other declaring all-out war, a prospect with the potential to rip Europe apart at the seams.

"It seems a shame that a treaty cannot be reached between them," I offer in a light tone. "War is such indelicate sport."

He frowns at my light remark.

"War is not sport, my lady."

I shrug. "Perhaps. But, in all this, a war began when two great powers disagreed over matters that should have been simple."

He lowers his chin, glowering at me. "I do not think you understand."

"I understand that there was a decree signed, one that should have been honored and was not. And then, another decree, another promise unkept. I know that because of this, the rightful heir was overlooked in succession and that there are those who will not willingly accept such a thing."

"That agreement was long undone."

"Perhaps. So which agreement should be held to? My thought would be the first. An oath made requires a leader who is honorable enough to keep it, despite any fleeting inconveniences that might arise. But then, perhaps I do not understand. I am only Prussian after all."

He frowns and sets his jaw.

"I think you are mistaken, Princess. Surely, you are as Russian as the empress herself is. I see it in your countenance. You may have been born elsewhere, but your heart is Russian."

Count Lestocq interrupts, taking me by the arm gently.

"Excuse me; I must speak with the princess."

I mumble my excuse and let him lead me away, as we pass the table a take a glass of wine and drink it quickly.

"Already making enemies with the English, are we?" he asks, his tone friendly.

I sigh. "He smelled of bitters and vodka and spit when he spoke."

Now my companion laughs heartily.

"Very true. But I suspect we will be rid of him soon. I expect the empress to side with France, though the chancellor would very much like to see a different outcome." He stops himself, as if realizing to whom he's speaking, and waves me off. "Not your concern. But, right now, I do have news that should concern you."

I take another drink, finishing off the chalice and setting it down as the wine begins to soften the edges of my mind.

"What news?" I ask, a bit afraid to hear the answer.

"We are expecting more company in only two days' time. Princess Charlotte of Saxony. She's coming at the chancellor's behest. No doubt as an attempt to undermine your engagement to Peter."

"There is no engagement. Not yet."

"And if Bestuzhev succeeds in offering her as an

alternative prospect, we could lose any chance of seeing that engagement happen."

I sit at a long bench near the hallway and motion for him to do the same.

"Tell me about her, what do you know?"

"She is a true Saxon princess, a daughter of King Augustus of Poland. She was all set to be wed to the next Dauphin of France before the battles began. Now they will send her to us, in the hopes that a union with Peter could turn Russia to their favor, against France."

"Yes, but what of her?"

He shrugs. "She's quite lovely, by all accounts. Well bred, versed in all things of the gentler nature. And if her mother is any indication, she will be more than capable of providing plenty of heirs. Sixteen children or something like that, her mother has."

He stretches warily, as if exhaustion has seeped into his very bones.

"But this, this is of the most importance to you. She will try to win Russia by winning Peter. Bestuzhev knows the empress' favor lies with you, only a very impassioned plea from Peter himself might change her mind."

I let that sink in. The empress would choose me, unless Peter loses his heart to another. She would put his happiness above her loyalty to my family—as she should. If I have any chance, I must have Peter securely in my hands before Charlotte arrives.

That doesn't give me much time.

"Can you do something for me?" I ask, a plan still formulating in the back of my mind.

He nods.

"Find the royal seamstress. Tell her I need a riding habit. By morning."

He looks at me, his expression curious.

"Apparently, I only have two days to win a war."

Chapter Six

The morning air is brisk; the last embers of fire glowing in my fireplace do little to stave off the chill. It's still dim, the sun only beginning to rise, yet there is a soft sound, the hum of a palace alive. I can already smell eggs and meats being prepared in the kitchens far below. I step quietly out of my bedchamber and into the sitting room. As good as her word, the seamstress has left a lovely red-and-gold riding habit for me. I run my fingers over the fine embroidery and buttons of the jacket. It's thick, heavy damask with coils of silk and lace in the bodice—much nicer than anything I've ever owned.

With a gentle tap at the door, the maid sweeps in. She curtsies.

"Pardon me, my lady. You have a visitor."

I stand, smoothing my hand down my dressing gown.

"Who is it?"

"It's Ricovi, the grand duke's valet."

She walks over and helps me into a long satin and

fur-lined robe that she's brought with her. When I'm covered, I take a seat.

"Show him in."

Ricovi is an older man with long, white hair coiled into rolls atop his head. He's in a tight blue suit and bows deeply as he enters the room. "My lady, I've been told to deliver this."

He holds out a simple, wooden box, which my maid takes and hands to me.

"A gift from His Highness, the prince," he adds with another bow.

I take the box and open it. Sitting on a bed of white satin rests a diamond-and-emerald tiara. Even in the dim light, the stones glow as if they are made of moonbeams and starlight.

"It's breathtaking. Please, send my deepest thanks to His Highness."

"Yes, my lady. And His Highness also wonders if you would care to join him for breakfast?"

I sit back, thinking over last night's events and the vague plan I've been forming in my mind.

"Please tell His Highness, that I would love to join him, but I have plans for an early morning ride. Tell him I'll meet him in the dining hall when I return."

The Valet looks mildly stunned at my refusal but bows and leaves the room.

As soon as he's gone, I call to the maid, "Quickly, send word to the groom to ready a horse for me. And send someone to rouse my ladies."

She nods, whispers to the guard outside my door, then comes back in to help me get ready.

I dress quickly and slide on a pair of riding boots—one of my few belongings they managed to retrieve from the woods—and brush my hair. I decide to leave it long and wavy, if only to feel the wind flow through it as I ride. My ladies appear soon after, both dressed and looking like they've been up for hours.

They curtsy, "My lady," they offer in unison.

"Good morning, I hope you both slept well."

Rina grins as Elizavetta wavers just a bit, her eyes droopy and her skin paler than I've seen it before.

"Some of us better than others," Rina says playfully, nudging her sister, who shoots her a rotten look.

"I'm going for a ride, and then we are to join His Highness for breakfast. Please see to it that I have a gown ready to wear and that some lavender and sage is brought up from the kitchens."

They nod, and I watch as the gesture makes Elizavetta grimace.

With a pang of sympathy, I add one more thing. "And Elizavetta, please go down to the kitchen and ask for a glass of spiced beer. If you drink it slowly, it will help the ache in your head."

Lord knows I've had to prepare the concoction enough times for my father after an argument with my mother left his temples pounding.

She nods gratefully. "Yes, my lady."

Writing a quick note to Mother, I head for the

stables.

The last remnants of the snow are vanishing quickly as the sun rises over the trees. In a few days it will be mostly gone—a mild winter to be sure. The ground under my feet is soft and wet as I make my way across the vast estate to the stables. Looking back over my shoulder, I see the entire palace begin to glow as if coming alive. The green-and-gold decorations over rows and rows of windows make it seem as if the palace is alive, with the promise of spring and growing things. Great marble statues surround the building, a large hedge obscuring only part of it from view.

Tearing my gaze from the finery, I walk quickly to the stables to find the groom there, and a beautiful chestnut mare waiting for me.

He holds out the reins, pleased by my expression. I run one gloved hand down her nose.

"She's beautiful," I say softly.

"Peony is her name. She's one of my finest."

I take the reins. "Thank you."

He nods and gently helps me into the saddle.

"Now, the best place to ride is just there in that open area in the courtyard."

I smile, with no intent of telling him my true destination.

"Thank you again. We will return shortly," I say

briskly, nudging her into a trot. I wait until I'm sure he's gone back into the tables before urging her to go a bit faster, and then a bit faster still.

We ride across the courtyard and into a thicket of trees. Peony seems pleased to be able to open up and run, and I don't have the heart to hold either of us back. Soon the trees open up a bit and we are in another field, this one wide and full of gently rolling hills. Finally, I slow her down. I can feel the strain on my face as the muscles widen, holding the large smile in place. I can't help it. It's the first time in months I've felt… free. As if out here, nothing can hold me down or hold me back. Soon I hear something, a dull thump as another set of hooves rides up behind me. I turn Peony quickly and come face to face with Peter, riding astride a tall, black horse of his own.

"I got your message," he says breathlessly as he trots up beside me. "It does seem like a nice day for a ride, doesn't it?"

I nod. "Yes, my lord. I've been cooped up for weeks; I just felt the need to… run for a bit."

He grins widely. "Yes, I know that feeling well."

I let my eyes flutter downward. His riding clothes are German in style, almost military looking with red-and-gold buttons and dark breeches. They make him look older, more like a general than a boy.

"Oh, and Happy Birthday. I don't think I got to say it last night."

He lowers his chin, flushing just a little.

"Yes, about that. I feel I owe you an apology. I behaved poorly."

I wave it off. "If we can't enjoy ourselves to excess once in a while, what is the value in life?"

"You aren't angry with me?" he asks, his tone becoming serious. I look up and see him watching my expression, trying to read my face as I respond.

"No, of course not. Should I be?"

His face frowns a little, and I can see he was hoping for something else.

"Though," I add quickly, "I was a bit disappointed I didn't get to spend more time with you. Perhaps more than a bit."

At that, he perks up, the boyish grin returning to his face. I grin too, only mine is a smile of relief. Somehow, I feel victorious. I've not only forced Peter to chase after me, but I've managed to express my feelings for him in a way that's not obsessive or dismissive. A delicate first strike in my counter attack, but a powerful one nonetheless.

"Well, why don't we ride for a bit?" he offers, leaning forward on his horse and patting its long, raven mane.

I raise one eyebrow in challenge. "I don't know, Peter. Do you think you can keep up?" With that, I'm off. Peony anticipates my desires as we move through the clearing back into the woods. Every turn, every jump, she's gliding through the forest as if she were born to it. A hawk more than a horse. I hear Peter close in behind me, and I pull her back just a bit. Soon we are neck and neck. I glance over and he's laughing, an expression of sheer joy plastered on his face. Passing in front of me, he rides ahead and then turns away. I follow, careful to stay close but not overtake him.

Before I know it, we're back on the palace grounds. As we break through the last of the thick woods, I see something happening in the courtyard. A dozen small fires have been lit in copper pans placed in a circle around a large rug, which has been spread out along the ground. A short table covered with food, milk, and wine sits in the center. There are large, lush sitting pillows scattered about. Beyond the ring of fires, my ladies and his lords stand, waiting for us to arrive.

Startled by the sight, I let Peony slow to a stop and stare at Peter, who has stopped a few feet in front of me and dismounted. A groom rushes over to take his horse, even as another walks briskly toward me. I let him help me dismount and hand him the reins, pulling off my warm, leather gloves.

Peter meets me halfway, holding out his arm.

"I decided to bring breakfast to us," he says proudly, as I take his arm and let him lead me to the feast he's created.

Peter walks up to the ring of fires and releases my arm to go greet his men. Rina and Elizavetta rush over to me, Elizavetta draping me in a warm, white, fur robe as Rina slides the tiara onto my head and combs through my wild hair with her fingers.

"Isn't it the most romantic thing?" Rina whispers.

"It's cold," Elizavetta complains softly, rubbing her hands together and blowing on them.

Peter returns, motioning for me to sit beside him.

"How was your ride this morning?" Alexander asks, taking a seat on Peter's other side.

"Brisk," I offer with a smile. "And quite what I needed."

"Most ladies don't ride in winter," Mikhail offers, passing a plate of food to Peter. "Especially alone."

Alexander interrupts, "But she wasn't alone, was she?"

"Certainly not. Lord Peter is much too chivalrous to make a lady ride alone," Elizavetta says, offering Peter a sweet smile, which sits ill with me. He raises his glass of wine and tilts his head, graciously accepting her compliment.

For the first time, something raises inside me, a feeling foreign and cold that I cannot quite place. I realize I do not like hearing his name on her lips.

Reaching over, I touch his hand gently.

"Yes, thank you for joining me. And thank you for this lovely gift." I lower my chin just a little so he can see I'm wearing it. Then I look up at him from beneath my eyelashes. "It's beautiful."

Reaching out, he lifts my chin, looking me full in the face.

"Yes, quite beautiful. As if were made to sit upon no other head," he says gently.

I feel myself blush at his words, and I don't try to conceal it.

Around us, the others begin to chat about the weather and the state of the budding war between England and France. I listen politely as I fill my plate and begin to eat. Every so often, out of the corner of my eye, I catch Peter watching me, his expression calm. Somehow, the topic turns to Elizavetta complaining that the royal seamstress is too busy to complete a new gown she's requested, and I feel the need to speak up.

"Yes, that's my fault, I'm afraid. All our things were destroyed in the attack, save a few items Mother was able to smuggle in her corset."

At that, the boys laugh.

"And you fought back? How terribly unladylike," Mikhail comments, his tone so level I can't tell if he's teasing. I decide to take his words lightly.

"A sentiment my mother shares, I assure you," I say.

"And what should she have done, Mikhail?" Alexander demands, his tone harsh. "Stepped out and stretched her neck so they could kill her without dirtying themselves?"

I feel my chest swell proudly as Alexander rushes to my defense. I offer him a grateful smile, which he returns.

Peter pipes in, "I quite agree. Savagery must be faced with savagery. Besides, I would have loved to see it, the lovely princess standing in the snow like a destroying angel."

"In her undergarments," Alexander mutters, and they burst out laughing again.

Peter's gaze slides over to me, a wide grin still spread across his face. "Enemies of Russia beware. Someday, Sophie will make a fierce queen."

I feel my throat tighten around the bit of cheese I've just swallowed.

It's the first time anyone has spoken of our marriage, even in a distant way. I'm surprised and not sure what to say to that. As I sit there, gaping at Peter like an idiot, Alexander saves me.

Holding up his glass of wine, he says, "To Princess Sophie. The someday queen of Russia."

The others join in and take a drink. By the time they are done, I've managed to recover myself, if only slightly.

"So Peter, will you stay here after your birthday celebrations are complete, or will you be off to Moscow?"

"I think I'll remain here. My aunt has ordered the construction of a new Winter Palace. I've seen the plans; it makes this one look like a peasant hut."

"That sounds amazing," Rina says, winding a tendril of yellow hair around her finger.

"It will be," Mikhail answers. "Would you like to see the plans? I've been helping the architects design the rooms. There's one made completely of green malachite and gold."

"That would be lovely," she says gently.

"Have you had a tour of the palace yet?" Alexander asks, taking a bite of bread.

I shake my head, "No, and I really should. I nearly got lost just making my way to the stables this morning. Perhaps you should draw me a map."

"I can do better than that," Peter interrupts. "I will give you the tour today. I will show you the new theater my aunt just installed. It will be part of tonight's festivities. And I could show you the trophy room if you're interested."

"That sounds wonderful. Have you added any trophies of your own yet?"

He frowns. "Most of them belong to my great uncle, but I plan to add a few of my own soon."

I smooth my skirt. "That sounds like great fun. I do love a good hunt. Perhaps I can join you sometime."

We wile away a few more hours in pleasant company until the sun is high in the sky and the food and wine are gone.

"I'm afraid I have an audience I must attend shortly," Peter says, standing up and offering me a hand. "More boring treaty discussions my aunt forces me to endure."

I stand beside him. "Of course. I'm sorry to have kept you so long," I say with a curtsy.

He takes my hand, still in his, and brings it to his lips quickly.

"Time moves far too swiftly in your company, Princess. Perhaps I can come by later, and we can have that tour? In say, two hours or so?"

"I look forward to it," I say honestly.

He jerks his head for Mikhail to join him, and the two walk off. Beside me, Alexander stands and offers me his arm, which I accept, and we begin walking back to the palace.

"Wouldn't want you to get lost on the way back to your rooms," he teases.

I sigh. "I actually have a very good sense of direction, you know."

"Oh yes, I can see that."

I lower my voice so the ladies following behind won't hear. "Thank you for your advice, about Peter."

He nods. "Anytime. I have to say, putting him off like that was brilliant. How did you know he'd come after you?"

"Just something I remember from when we were children. He always loved playing chase. And as for the ride, that was a happy accident. I really did need to clear my thoughts. That he chose to ride after me was a bit of a surprise."

"Not much of one though?"

I shake my head. "Peter loves to play and hates to lose. I don't think that's changed much over the years. As you said, it's just a game."

"I must ask then, is your affection for him genuine?" he asks boldly.

"What a thing to ask," I fire back. "Peter is an old friend, and possibly, might someday be my husband. Of course I have affection for him."

"And do you love him?"

I open my mouth to say something, but come up at a loss. Do I love Peter? Perhaps. Yet when he kissed my hand, I felt… nothing. None of the longing or intensity I've read about in books, not even the tiny stirrings I get around Sergei and Alexander. Perhaps those things are just fiction. Perhaps love is simply trust. Alexander is staring at me intently.

"You shouldn't ask me such things. It's rude."

"My apologies then."

I lick my lips. "Besides, there are many kinds of love."

"I'm sure that's true."

His words are hollow, complacent. I have a nagging urge to explore the topic further, but I can't bring myself to and I'm not sure why. Surely, he's been in love before. Wouldn't he know? As if sensing my questions, he continues.

"I think that love can indeed be many things. But the one thing it will never be is practical. Love is irrational by its very nature. It demands passion, fire, and no less than absolute surrender. It is a longing, a burning that consumes you, leaving you without reason, or defense. When love comes, nothing can stand in its way."

I say nothing for a minute, letting his words absorb

into my skin. Is that want I want, to be consumed by love? To have someone so desperate for me that they are beyond reason? And to be that desperate for someone else?

"That sounds… like a terrible way to die," I decide.

Beside me, he says nothing, but we keep walking. He stops every so often to orient me inside the palace.

Finally, we reach my door. My ladies go in ahead but I stop, turning to face him. His green-gold eyes are locked on mine—full of unspoken intentions. In that moment, the distance between us seems less like a few steps and more like a great chasm, as if he were so far away that I would have to call out so he might hear my voice.

"Thank you, Alexander," I mutter weakly.

He cocks his head to the side thoughtfully. "For what?"

My heart races again, and I am left wondering if what I felt between us had been more than just wine and dancing. Even now, here, part of me wonders what his hand would feel like on the small of my back, what his lips would taste like. I shake myself from the thoughts.

Not sure what to say, I turn and go inside without answering his question, closing the door between us. I realize that I'm flushed, breathing too quickly. It takes all my effort to drive the dark, handsome Alexander and his imaginary kisses out of my mind.

Chapter

Mother is gone when we arrive. A note tells me she is in meetings with Count Lestocq all afternoon. I breathe a deep sigh of relief at her absence. The maids bring up a few bowls of hot water, and my ladies help me strip down and wash before lacing me into one of my new gowns.

"How is she creating them so quickly?" I ask, not really expecting an answer.

"The empress has an army of women down in the sewing rooms working on them," Elizavetta says curtly. "By the end of the week, you'll have a closet full of new gowns."

"The empress is very kind," I say gently.

Rina agrees. "That she is. And she's quite fond of you."

"Of my family," I correct her.

"Oh, I don't think it's just that," she says. "And Lord Peter certainly seems smitten."

Elizavetta snorts, and I frown.

"Men can be quite fickle in their attentions. And

quite cruel to delicate hearts," I say, looking her in the eye. "You understand my position here, don't you?"

Elizavetta raises her chin boldly, her words like knives. "I understand that if you are unfit to wed Peter, another must be chosen."

I nod slowly. "And you must also realize that Peter will marry to secure an alliance, either with Prussia or Austria. Even now, there is a Saxon princess on her way to the palace to vie for his hand. Which of us wins will be determined by the empress and which country she chooses to make a treaty with. But either way, it will be one of us."

I say the words as gently as I can, but sternly enough so she realizes she's not a second option, but a distant third at best.

"You must understand, my lady." Rina steps forward as Elizavetta backs away, her eyes swimming with unshed tears. "Since we were children, our parents have been bringing us to court. As soon as Peter was made heir, they began grooming Elizavetta as a potential bride for him. She's been told that she was high in his esteem. Last night at the ball, when he lavished such attention on her, she thought…"

I nod. "You thought he would go against his empress, choosing to marry for love and not politics." I hold out my hand to Elizavetta and she takes it hesitantly, her already-round face puffy and red with emotion. "It is the dream of all women to marry a man we are deeply in love with, who is deeply in love with us. But we must also be practical." Even as the words escape my mouth, I hear Alexander's voice in my head.

Love is never practical.

I brush the thought aside. "Sometimes, we must learn to open our hearts and grow to love someone we think we might not be able to. It's the lot of women, especially noble women. We are little more than property, bargaining chips, or chains that hold alliances together. That is the price we pay for our comfort, riches, and titles."

She snatches her hand away. "But you will get both. You will get to marry a man you love, who loves you in return. What makes you so special?"

Her words are like a slap in the face. I stand and she takes a small step back, as if she thinks I might strike her.

"I assure you that if I marry Peter, I will love him because I will be his wife and that will be my duty. Not because of some silly, childish sentiment or romantic fantasies."

She stares at me, her eyes wide.

"Then you do not love him at all." She challenges. I'm not sure how to respond so I wave her off.

"Go down and tell the seamstress I've ordered you to get a new gown. Tell her you need it urgently, at my request."

She curtsies and bolts from the room, leaving Rina and me alone. I slump down in my chair.

"I didn't mean to be cruel," I say softly, as Rina begins to brush my hair.

"I know, my lady. And Elizavetta will come to understand. She's a silly girl, always imagining herself madly in love with someone or other. Once it was a stable boy named Benjamin. Father nearly had a stroke when he found out."

"I can imagine."

"The worst part was that the poor boy had no idea. He genuinely thought she had taken up an interest in horses."

I laugh.

"I will try not to be too hard on her. It's not her fault after all; Peter is a terrible flirt."

At that, my guard enters the room. "My lady, General Salkov to see you."

Sergei steps into the room. Though he's only a few years older than I am, he carries himself like a true man, tall and confident. There's a hint of stubble along his jaw still, and he bows deeply, offering me a warm smile that makes his eyes crinkle in the corners. His arms are full of books and papers.

"Princess, I thought we might continue your lessons today."

"Of course," I say, nodding to Rina. She takes her cue, wandering to the far corner of the room with a bit of embroidery while Sergei and I sit.

We go over a few basic greetings, he reads a few passages from Paradise Lost, and then I repeat them.

He corrects me, and we repeat them again until I've got the pronunciation correct. When we finish, he snaps the book closed with one hand, turning his body so he is facing me, though we are sitting very close.

"It's nice to see you, Sergei," I say honestly. He's one of the few people in the palace I feel like I can really trust. Even my own mother seems to be keeping something from me, not a fact, just a feeling I get when I see her scurry in and out of the chambers. But something about Sergei puts me completely at ease, as if I could tell him anything, and he would still be on my side.

Maybe it's just wishful thinking, but Sergei is more than a friend. He's my ally.

"And you, Princess. I hear you've had an eventful morning."

I nod. "I had a ride, and then breakfast with Peter. It was quite a surprise." I bow my head just a bit. "And he gave me this lovely gift."

Sergei smiles. "Good. I assume Count Lestocq told you about our expected guest from the south?"

I nod again. "He did."

"Sophie, there are a few things we need to discuss. First, before you can marry Peter, there are a few matters you must attend to."

"Like what?"

"Foremost, you will need to convert to the Orthodox Church."

I feel a wave of nausea wash over me. My father

is a devout Lutheran. My whole family is, myself included. It was the only thing he asked of me when he agreed to allow me to travel here, that I keep his faith. To convert would be like turning my back on him. I lower my head into my hands.

"Is there no other way?"

He reaches his hand out and places it on the back of my neck. His touch is firm but gentle, his hands soft but strong. Even though he's very warm, the places where he touches me are chilled.

"They aren't such different faiths. Fundamentally the same actually. I will have Bishop Todorskey come speak to you. He confesses the empress herself. Perhaps he can ease your worries."

I look up at him. His green eyes are deep with concern.

"My father will never speak to me again if I do this."

"And you know what will happen if you refuse."

I close my eyes, forcing myself to breathe in and out calmly. The reminder is unnecessary. I know well the cost of my failure. My family's name, their very existence, is at stake, and it weighs on my shoulders every moment.

"What else?"

He sits back, releasing me.

"There is a matter of some delicacy in the next two things. The first is a test. The court physician must verify… your virtue."

I feel my mouth drop open.

"Verify how?"

He flushes, looking down at his boots.

"It is a procedure that all potential royal wives must endure. You cannot come to the royal bed unless you are fully intact. I'd hoped to have your mother discuss this with you, but she seems quite occupied. It's a simple thing, really."

"It sounds awful."

"Don't be afraid, Sophie. You know I would never harm you or allow anyone else to harm you. You trust me in this, don't you?"

I stare at him for a minute. He had risked his life to ride out and protect me, late though he was, and he was here now, preparing me for the things that must be done.

"I do," I say finally.

He breathes a sigh of relief. "Good. The final thing you will do, well, they are lessons of a sort. With Madame Groot."

"What kind of lessons? Language?"

"No. Something of a more personal nature. The empress herself has demanded it. You see, she needs not just an heir for herself, but to secure the dynasty, she needs Peter to have an heir also, and as quickly as possible."

I blink rapidly.

"I don't understand."

"There are ways… for a woman to…" He stops,

rubbing his eyes with his thumb and middle finger. "Lord, how I wish I didn't have to say these things—not to you. Madame Groot is going to tutor you in the wifely arts."

At his words, I leap to my feet.

"What sickness is this? You would have me trained as a whore? Is Russian court so depraved? I will not consent. Not to this. How humiliating."

He stands, taking my arms in his hands and stepping close.

Too close. Our bodies are nearly pressed together. I can feel his breath on my face and neck and it feels—good. Too good, I realize. I put a hand on his chest to steady myself, and I can feel his own heartbeat pick up speed under my fingers. My heart jumps as he whispers into my hair.

"Learning to please your husband is not depraved or sick. A man has needs. If you cannot meet them, he will tire of you quickly. I assure you, the lessons will be academic, not practical. Many young ladies have tutored with Madame Groot, and none have been shamed by it. But you are young, beautiful, and naïve to the wiles you possess, to the way even your subtle gestures and words affect the men around you. Your feminine nature will be one of your greatest weapons, but it must be honed, and you must be taught to wield it."

I look up at him, our faces only inches apart. Why do all these Russian men have to be so devastatingly, frustratingly handsome?

"You speak of me as if I possess a sword, and swing it recklessly." My voice cracks, unable to contain the tidal wave rolling in my belly.

"You are the sword," he whispers, releasing me and stepping back. I nearly stumble, because my legs have gone weak. I have to turn away from him, wrapping my arms around myself to calm my shaking.

"Fine. See to it then," I say, managing with great effort to hold my voice steady.

"And you will be attending the banquet tonight, I presume?"

I nod, my back still to him.

"Of course."

"May I make a suggestion?"

I slide my hands down my bodice before turning back to him.

He hesitates, a flush rising to his cheeks. "Perhaps, you might consider the red gown this evening. The color flatters you greatly."

"I will consider it. Thank you."

He clicks his heels together and bows, leaving the room slowly, pausing once to glance back at me. As soon as he's out the door, I relax and Rina hurries to my side.

"He's right, you know, about Madame Groot," she offers, pouring me a glass of wine and holding it out to me.

I raise an eyebrow, and she blushes. "She's well

known and very respected at court. Her husband was a great general and when he passed away, she took many lovers. Eventually, the wealthy and privileged began to seek out her counsel on everything from infertility to how to guarantee a child would be male."

"It seems like everything here at court is managed in some way or another," I say before taking a sip. "I dislike being managed."

She smiles bashfully, her slender face flushing.

'I assume you overheard everything?" I ask lightly. She blushes again and nods softly. "Good. I need someone who knows when to keep their ears open. So you know I have some competition arriving tomorrow. Princess Charlotte of Saxony. "

"And she seeks a marriage as well?"

"She does. And more than that, Chancellor Bestuzhev will be pressing for it. He is close to the empress, and she relies heavily on his counsel." I sit and motion for her to do the same. "Of course, I have Sergei on my side, and that is a great advantage. But perhaps not quite enough."

"Sergei has the empress' ear, surely. They were lovers once, though now just friends."

I feel my mouth fall open. I'd been unaware of their relationship. But looking at Sergei, I can certainly understand it. Though he is far younger than she is, he has a very rugged, manly cut about him. And he is infallibly charming. As I think upon him, an image of him appears in my mind. I push it away. He is my friend, yes, I am comfortable calling him such, and my advisor. I appreciate his counsel and his help. Beyond that, there can be nothing.

I continue, "My only chance is to make certain Peter is so enamored of me that he doesn't even look in her direction. I think you can help me with that."

She smiles warmly. "Of course, anything I can do."

"Tonight, after the banquet, I am going for an evening stroll around the palace. It would do well if Peter were not too drunk to join me, so please have the kitchen staff water down his wine. Then tomorrow morning, have the maids set up an archery station in the meadow near the west wing just after sunrise, so that it will be visible from his window."

"I can do that," she agrees, just as the door swings open and Mother breezes into the room. She's wearing a new gown—one of the ones the seamstress made for me—a golden brocade with yellow lace and black buttons that is so tight across her chest I'm surprised she hasn't burst out of it. Her hair is tall, curled in rings, and powdered white, and she's drawn a small beauty mark on her left cheek. Over all, she looks quite comical.

"Mother, what have you been up to this fine day?" I ask, trying to keep my tone light.

She pulls a lace fan from her sleeve and begins fanning herself quickly.

"I have been securing our family's fortune. And what have you been doing?"

I straighten my back. "I took lessons with Sergei today, and we discussed a few other things as well. He is arranging for me to speak to a cardinal about conversion. Did you know that would be a requirement of marriage to Peter?" I know I shouldn't ask, that it might upset her, but I can't help the nagging feeling that she's known quite a bit more about all this than she let on.

As I expect, she waves me off. "It's all the same thing really. Nothing to prickle yourself over."

"Father will be devastated," I say gently.

She snaps, slapping the fan closed in her hand. "That is precisely why your father was not invited to take this journey with us. He's too stubborn for his own good." She pauses, looking at me, and her tone softens, "Don't worry. Once he sees how greatly this union will benefit him, he will have only good wishes to send your way. Why, the King of Prussia has already sent him a chest of gold and increased his lands two fold. Imagine the favors he will lavish upon your family once you are the Empress Consort of Russia!"

I try to smile, but it's hollow. Of course, I want my father to be happy and have his lands and title secure; I only wish I didn't have to sell my soul to Russia to do it.

Mother excuses herself to go have tea with the empress while Rina and I begin a game of chess. Soon, Elizavetta interrupts us.

She curtsies.

"My lady, I must apologize for my behavior before, and for the way I acted last night. I meant you no disrespect."

Her face is still red and puffy, though it looks as if she's tried to cover it with powder. I smile, patting the seat next to me.

"Of course I forgive you. Here, sit with me and watch as I thoroughly defeat Rina in this battle of wits."

She takes her seat, relaxing into the chair beside me.

We finish our game, which I am almost certain Rina allows me to win, then the girls scuttle off to make the arrangements I've asked for. Two maidservants arrive with the seamstress as she delivers my gown for the evening. They set it across my bed and leave just as my page announces my visitor.

"His Lordship Peter von Holstein-Gottorp," the young man announces just before Peter strides into my chamber. He's changed into a pale green suit and breeches with golden trim. His hair is combed back tightly into a small tail at the back of his neck.

He bows.

"Princess, I have come to give you the tour as promised."

Peter holds out his arm to me, his face serene, if a bit pink from our earlier time in the sun. I smile warmly and accept his gesture, locking my arm around his and allowing him to lead me from the room.

He begins recounting the discussion from his earlier meeting as we wind down elaborate corridor after corridor. He leads me past the library without pausing. I crane my neck to catch a fleeting glimpse of the room as we pass quickly, but I don't ask to stop. His pace is quick, a man with a destination in mind to be sure.

"How are the lessons going with General Salkov?" he asks pointedly.

"Quite well, thank you. He is a wonderful teacher."

Peter stops, raising his hand, "Make no mistake; he has my aunt's interests at heart, not ours."

As he says the word ours, he motions to the two of us, as if we are co-conspirators in some great plot. I force a smile, unsure what to say.

He continues walking and adds, “It’s not that I have anything against the man, to be sure. But there is a general tone about him that I dislike. An arrogance, perhaps. If I thought for a moment that his lessons with you had been in any way inappropriate…”

His words trail off but his tone is clear. He feels threatened by the handsome general. I quickly work to set him at ease.

“No need to worry there, he’s been nothing but a gentleman. I think he is much too smart to attempt any such nonsense.”

He offers a satisfied grunt. “Good. I know my aunt is fond of him and I’d hate to see how she would react if I were to have to punish him.”

His words chill me to the core. I’ve never heard Peter sound so cold and harsh before.

As soon as we turn the next corner, I know where he’s leading me. The great hall is lined with suits of armor, tall pedestals of marble displaying all manner of weapons, and in the very center is a stone statue of his namesake, Peter the Great. He leads me past each display, describing their bloody lineage in vivid detail. I nod, feigning interest. Some of the battles he describes I’ve read about in books, others are wholly unheard of to me.

When he was a child, Peter had a set of toy soldiers that were his dearest possessions. He’d loved nothing more than recreating his favorite battles. His obsession, it seems, has only grown.

With a sudden burst of gusto, he leaps atop a chair and pulls an old pair of crossed swords from their places on the wall. He flips on in his hand, grabbing it by the dull blade and holds it out to me.

"Here, Princess. How about a real lesson?"

I take the hilt warily.

"What are you doing?" I ask in a whisper. "Surely we aren't meant to use these."

He offers me a wicked smirk, and then raises his sword.

"Prepare to defend yourself, Prussia!" he screams and advances. I manage to swing the heavy sword just in time to block his blow.

Encouraged by my move he continues, circling me like a predator, sword firm in his grasp. I watch him move, trying to emulate his posture.

In an instant, he lunges and I am only barely able to spin out of his way. He laughs and I can hardly keep the irritation off of my face. Thinking back to all the times I'd played wooden swords with my father I place one hand in the small of my back and swing the blade, drawing his attention to my left as I step forward and lunge half-heartedly. He blocks my move easily. Our swords come together with a loud clang and he takes his free hand and grabs me, pulling me to him until we are pressed together, only the cold steel between us. I push back and prepare to defend myself.

"Put the tip higher," he orders, moving again.

"Keep your weight on your back foot."

He circles me, barking commands.

"Lunge!" he orders and I obey, trying to look more uncoordinated that I really am. I do manage to trip on the hem of my massive skirts and fall forward just a little. Though I catch myself before I fall, the maneuver gives Peter enough time to come up behind me and slap my backside with the flat part of his sword. Though I really can't feel it through the layers of pannier and skirt I give a little yelp of surprise. I look over my shoulder to see a wide, devilish grin set in his face. A sense of unease fills me in that moment that I cannot quite explain to myself. Peter doesn't look malevolent, but something in his expression reminds me of a child who has recently discovered a new toy.

The sound of trumpets blaring behind us startles me, making me jump. Peter turns away from me, looking curiously down the hall.

I'm glad he's not watching me because I feel my expression fall, my expression souring.

Princess Charlotte of Saxony has arrived early.

Peter replaces our swords and then, taking me by the arm, he leads me back through the maze of corridors and to the main staircase. Four more trumpets blare and drummers beat their drums. The empress sweeps into the room from my right, descending the steps in front of us. Chancellor Bestuzhev and Count Lestocq meet her at the massive palace doors.

We flood outside just in time to see a white-and-gold sleigh pull to the front, tall, purple banners flowing behind it. The sleigh is pulled by an army of white horses so lovely that they could be made of snow and ice.

The sleigh stops and four people climb out, three young ladies and one young man. The young man steps forward, and they all bow and curtsy before the empress. I spot Princess Charlotte immediately. Her large, flowing gown is deep purple, nearly black. It perfectly accents her hair, though I don't think black describes the color. Her hair is raven, the color of midnight, and her eyes are just as dark. Her lips are large and puffy like Elizavetta's, only, somehow, they sit just right on her face. In every possible way, this new princess is stunningly, breathtakingly beautiful. As she walks forward, taking the young man's arm, I glance over at Peter. He's watching her impassively, as if her beauty hasn't reached his eyes yet. Then he looks over at me and winks. Raising my hand in his, he grazes a kiss across my knuckles before releasing me to join his aunt.

I release a long breath, feeling myself relax at his reaction.

The young man bows again as they reach the empress.

"Your Majesty. I am Hans Svetten, Duke of Dresden, Saxony. I would like to present my sister, Princess Charlotte, and her ladies."

Charlotte curtsies deeply.

"Your Majesty," she offers in a rich, deep voice.

"Welcome to St Petersburg. I am overjoyed you could make the journey," the empress responds coolly. "This is my nephew, Grand Duke Peter von Holstein-Gottorp."

Peter bows, but he does not extend his hand. I feel my shoulders straighten, my chin raise, all without conscious thought. The empress, probably sensing Peter's apathy, motions to the chancellor. "Please, Chancellor Bestuzhev will show you to your apartments."

Without waiting, Peter turns his back to the princess and her entourage, walks toward me, and offers his arm, which I take without hesitation. The empress spares us only a quick glance over her shoulder, but I think I see a sly smile curl across her lips.

As soon as we are out of earshot, Peter leans down and whispers into my ear.

"If Bestuzhev thinks he can control the alliance by controlling my heart, he is sadly mistaken. No one controls me."

I raise one eyebrow. "Not even the empress?"

He chuckles. "Not even the empress."

That night at the banquet, the room is very clearly divided. The empress sits at the head of the table,

Sergei to her left and Bestuzhev at her right. Princess Charlotte and her brother sit beside the chancellor. I sit on Sergei's other side with my mother beside me. A few other dignitaries fill the remaining seats and Peter is at the other end of the table, chatting with Mikhail and Alexander, who flank him.

"How was your journey?" Sergei asks Charlotte politely.

"Lovely," she responds automatically, staring down the table to Peter. "Russia is truly a lovely country."

Peter snorts and raises a glass of wine.

"Russia is a truly cold country, at least this time of year."

He inclines his glass in my direction before taking a long drink. Setting the cup down, he frowns.

"This wine is terrible," he winks at me, "must be Portuguese."

I grin at the remark.

"And how are you enjoying your time at court?" Charlotte asks me pointedly. "It's your first time here, isn't it?"

I smile. "It is my first time in Russia, though I met Peter years ago at Swedish court. We were actually good friends as children." It's a slight exaggeration, but Peter doesn't correct me so I continue, "And I have been having a wonderful visit. Only today, His Highness surprised me with the most beautiful breakfast picnic."

I watch her face and see her smile slip, just a

touch, before she takes a bite of food. A roar of pride fills me, followed immediately by guilt. I should not be so cruel. She is only a girl, like myself, being used as a pawn in a much larger game. Under any other circumstances, we might even be friends. But here, in this court, we are rivals.

And we must each do whatever it takes to win.

Turning to the empress, I continue.

"Sergei has set a meeting with the cardinal tomorrow so we can discuss my conversion," I say boldly. Truthfully, I hadn't yet decided to go through with it, but as soon as the empress hears the words, she rewards me with a warm smile. I know there can be no changing my mind now.

"That's excellent."

At the end of the table, Peter snorts. "I see my aunt has convinced you of the merits of Orthodoxy. Congratulations," he says bitterly. "She tried to convince me to do the same, but I refused."

I glance quickly at Sergei, who doesn't meet my eye.

Recovering as best I can, I simply say, "Being the future king has its benefits, I suppose."

After dinner, we retire to the massive theater where the empress has staged a production of *Ariadne*—a respite from her preferred entertainment of Italian Opera, Peter assures me. Peter is flanked by his men, as always, but motions for me to take a seat next to Alexander. I almost feel bad for Charlotte.

She smiles warmly, trying to catch Peter's eye, but he looks right past her. I watch the smile slip off her face, replaced by a confused frown. I doubt any man has ever looked beyond her in such a manner. It's his man, Mikhail, who finally steps in and offers the princess and her brother a seat beside him. She looks grateful, her brother, however, looks completely put out as he takes his seat.

The lamps are put out as the stage lights are lit. Immediately, the room is thrown into shadows as the first actors appear.

And the play is in Russian, of course.

I sigh deeply and sit back, watching as a man in yellow brocade struts across the stage. In the darkness, Alexander leans over and whispers.

"You don't speak Russian, do you?"

I shake my head silently.

He leans in closer. "Then I will translate for you," he offers softly.

Alexander leans over, his shoulder grazing mine. In the darkness, the gesture seems too intimate, too deliberate. "He is narrating, saying that Theseus has killed the Minotaur and now he and Ariadne have fled to the island of Naxos, to the protection of King Oenarus."

The narrator steps off stage and the long, golden curtains open to reveal a young woman's room. She's weeping in the arms of another woman. They exchange words in a sad, rushed conversation. One strokes the other's long, brown hair and soothes her softly and begins a low, wistful aria

"The one crying," I say quietly. "She's Ariadne?"

Alexander nods. "She's upset because she's in love with Theseus, but he has refused to marry her. The other girl is her sister, Phaedra."

The play goes on, each character draped in nearly sheer togas, garlands of ivy upon their heads. It would be quite indecent, except for the art of it. Though I don't understand what's being said, I am able to follow the story very well—a testament to the skill of the actors.

"I don't understand. If Theseus is in love with Phaedra, and she with him, why don't they just tell Ariadne? Surely, she would understand?" I ask quietly to Alexander.

"Because, they both care about Ariadne. They want her to accept the love of the king and find happiness before they tell her, for fear that the truth would destroy her," he explains.

"Do they really think it would hurt her so badly?"

He chuckles softly. "Spoken like one who has never been on the wrong side of unrequited love. This line she just spoke, she said to Theseus, *Of the entire universe, I only wanted you.*"

I watch as the poor, star-crossed lovers flee the kingdom and, in despair at her lost love's betrayal, Ariadne sings a sad melody and then falls on her sword. The curtain closes. I feel the moisture roll from my eye just as the valets re-light the wall lamps.

"Are you crying, princess?" Alexander asks, offering me a hand to my feet.

I wipe the tear away but another falls in its place. "It's so devastating. The pain and the suffering, and for what? It strikes me to my very soul."

"Ariadne believed that without love, life had no meaning. Killing herself spared her a lifetime of heartache."

I shake my head. "That's idiocy. She didn't stop the pain, she only handed off her chance to make things better. She could have found love again. It was a waste."

He snickers.

"You take the story too closely to your heart, I think," he says. Reaching up, he wipes a newly fallen tear from my cheek. The touch is so quick and gentle that for a moment, I think I might have imagined it.

I look up to find his green eyes staring at me, as if they could peer through my flesh into my soul. I want to hold his gaze, but it's too overpowering, like staring into the noonday sun, and I have to look away.

My next words catch in my throat. Even looking away, I can feel the weight of his stare on me. The flush fills my face with heat, adding to my embarrassment.

"Perhaps you're right," I manage finally.

Reaching around Alexander, Peter takes my hand. "Come, Princess. I will see you safely to your room," he offers.

Alexander steps back and lets me pass in front of him. The empress turns to us, giving Peter a quick jerk of the chin, gesturing to Charlotte. He pauses only for a moment to incline his head to the princess.

"Good evening," he says quickly, leading me out into the foyer.

"What did you think of the production?" I ask as we make our way down the hall, my ladies and his men falling in step behind us.

He leans over, his voice barely a whisper. "I thought it was dreadfully boring. I think something with a little more action and less prose would be more entertaining."

"Perhaps," I mutter halfheartedly. I thought the play was quite enjoyable, despite not being able to understand the words. But then Peter was never much for the arts.

"All these formal balls and plays. This court seriously lacks the more masculine entertainments. When I am king, we will have tournaments like in old days. Jousting, swordplay, and archery. And we will have formal military drills every day. These are the things that make a country strong. Not dance and theater." He pauses. "It will be more like King Fredrick's court."

I pat his hand gently. "Surely arts and poetry will have its place as well. Those are the things that nurture the soul."

He looks at me, his face stern and serious. "I worry

less about the soul of Russia and more about its might. Times are changing, and we must be on firm footing before the tide of change rolls our way."

I smile softly. "All the world's a stage, and all the men and women merely players."

He stops. "Why do you say that?"

"It's from a poem by Shakespeare. You've heard of his work?"

He shakes his head. "Reading gives me terrible head pain. Especially when the author is English."

He laughs, and I hear others behind us join in. I try to hide the disappointment that weighs on me. Books are one thing I love above all else. In a story, I can become anyone, travel any place. In those pages lives my only true freedom.

We stop at my door, and my ladies open it. I curtsy to Peter, who bows, taking my hand.

"Farewell, sweet Sophie. I hope to see you again soon," he says with a flourish.

"Sleep well, Peter," I offer, leaving him to his friends.

As soon as the door closes, my mother enters from her private chamber.

"How was the play?" she asks with cool disinterest.

"It was delightful," I offer. "Which you would have known if you'd been in attendance. Where on earth did you get off to?"

She waves her hand, as if it doesn't matter at all. "I was feeling ill, so I retired early."

I narrow my eyes suspiciously and look her over. Her cheeks are flushed, her lips plump. She doesn't look ill at all, and from experience, if she had fallen ill, she surely would have made quite a show of it. No, something is strange about her, and though I can't quite place it, I'm certain she's lying.

"Mother, please. I know something has you stirred up. Can you not tell me what it is?"

She presses a finger to her lips and waves me over, lowering her voice to a whisper.

"Kind Fredrick has tasked me with keeping him apprised of the goings on here at court. I am his personal correspondent."

I feel myself recoil.

"You mean spy?"

She waves me off.

"Nothing so indelicate. I am a representative of Prussia; it is my solemn duty to keep him apprised of what I see here."

I bite my bottom lip. There is a stiff penalty for spying and if she's discovered…

"You are putting both our positions here in great jeopardy. I must insist that you stop this madness at once." I demand.

She straightens, her face pulling into a frown.

"Do not presume to order me about, little one. You aren't queen yet. I suggest you worry less about me and more about what will happen to you if you fail to secure an engagement."

Her words are like ice, filling me with dread.

"Yes, Mother," I say through clenched jaw.

With a firm nod, she turns and leaves, closing her door behind her.

With a resigned heart, I let my ladies help me out of my gown and into my nightdress. I dismiss them for the evening, and a maid brings me up a tray of warm milk. When I take a sip, I notice there is a small, folded parchment under my cup. I pick it up quickly, clutching it to my chest as I make my way to my private room. Sitting on the edge of my lush bed, I unfold the letter.

They have their exits and their entrances, and one man in his time plays many parts.
Meet me in the library at midnight.

I wad up the note in my hand and clutch it to my chest. From my open window, I hear the bells at St. Peter's Cathedral chime out the hours. Eleven clear, deep bell strikes echo through my chamber.

I open the paper up and read it again. It's the next verse from the Shakespeare poem I had quoted to Peter earlier. Had he been feigning his distaste of poetry? Had he been teasing me? Perhaps I have misjudged him. After all, he is no longer the boy I remember. He's a man, groomed to be a king. I look down at my hands, waiting for some feeling of excitement. But all that comes is a wash of relief. Peter has chosen me, and all my family's problems will be solved. My father will keep his land and my brother his title, even Mother will never want for anything ever again. No more second-season gowns or scraping by. Her dream for me has come true. So why do I, deep in my heart, feel nothing but cold detachment?

I chew on my bottom lip as I read the words over and over, trying to ferret out any possible hidden meaning. Going out at such an hour seems so… rebellious. That is a side to Peter I wasn't aware of. I have to admit, the idea that there may be more to him, well, it excites my curiosity. Perhaps I simply need to give it time, to allow my feelings for him to grow as I get to know him in the small, secret ways only a wife can know a husband. I allow the flicker of hope to grow, giving me something to cling to. Still, wandering around the palace in the middle of the night is risky at best, what would people say if I were found out? What would my mother say?

Carefully holding the paper to the flame of my flickering bedside candle, I watch as it burns, dropping it on the marble floor just as it turns to ash. Walking to my window, I stare out, the cold night air blowing across my face, stirring my long, loose hair. I close my eyes, imagining the wind is his fingers, touching my face, stroking my hair. Only the image I conjure isn't Peter, but another. For the briefest moment, I lose myself in the daydream, the scent of him, the feel of his body pressed against mine as we dance. I look at his full lips and wonder what they would feel like, dancing their way across my flesh. My eyes snap open, and I push the dream away. I can't afford thoughts like that, dangerous, errant desires for a man who will never be mine.

The city below is silent, held in the grip of night. Only the sliver of moonlight reflecting on the rooftops sets it aglow. It's eerily still, frozen in time. Reaching out, I pull the window closed and turn the lock. The city may be sleeping soundly, but I have never felt more awake.

I slip into a simple gown and wait. As soon as I hear the first bell chime, I sneak through the dark room and out the door. My guard has long since retired for the evening and won't be back until nearly dawn.

The hall is quiet; each footstep I take echoes like thunder, along with the sound of my drawing breath, which to my nervous ears is much, much too loud. My heart races, pounding against my chest like a hammer striking an anvil. I get turned around only once before finding my way through the maze of halls to the library. I can see lights flickering under the door, so I push it open slowly.

Once inside, I'm flooded with golden lamplight. The room is tall, two floors with a large, wooden staircase in the center of the room, with books stacked floor to ceiling. The exposed walls are stark white with gold inlay, the Romanov crest—the double-headed eagle—appears all around the room, carved into every surface, ceiling to table. There are two long, rectangular tables decorated with vases of fresh flowers and marble busts and various golden chairs and settees litter the room. I look up, and the domed canopy above me is painted with a lovely sky fresco, giving the illusion that the room is open to the heavens.

But what draws me in, what gives me a sense of calm, is the smell. That marvelous scent of paper and leather fills the room. I inhale deeply, letting the familiar smell carry me away. Crossing to the nearest shelf, I run my hand along the row of spines, enjoying the texture under my fingers. A noise above me startles me from my tactile reverie.

"You'd think you've never seen a library before."

Chapter Nine

My heart leaps into my throat. At the top of the stairs is Alexander. He's still wearing his formal suit, his dark hair slightly disheveled as always. For a heartbeat, I'm too stunned to speak. It's as if my deepest desires have been formed to flesh. If not for the rush of blood to my face, I might think I was dreaming.

When I finally regain my wits, I have to look away, swallowing heavily before I speak.

"Alexander, I did not expect to see you this evening."

I hear his heavy boots bound down the steps.

"I understand. You must have thought my note was from Peter. I apologize for disappointing you."

He crosses the room, standing close enough for me to feel the air around me stir with his presence.

"I admit I did think they were Peter's words." Though hoped is more accurate. I don't tell him that it isn't disappointment coursing through my veins, but joy. Sheer, terrible, frightening joy. I clear my throat, knowing I can never say such things to him. "I never suspected you would be so rude as to proposition me in such an inappropriate manner."

Without looking at him, I turn, ready to run back to my room but also steeling myself against his absence. When had my own feelings become so muddled and complicated? Before I take a single step, he catches my arm, turning me to him.

"I apologize for the misunderstanding, but please know it was never my intention to proposition you in any way. I needed to speak to you privately. This seemed the best way."

Without meaning to, I look up and catch his eye. His expression is solemn and sincere.

"Please," he adds gently.

I nod my head just a fraction of an inch. I doubt I could deny him anything when he's looking at me like that. I pull away, afraid he might hear my heart gain speed, racing at his simple touch.

Stepping forward, he slides a book from the shelf and hands it to me. I glance at the cover. It's a book of poetry by Sir Walter Raleigh. I hand it back, determined to hide the emotions raging inside me.

"I prefer something less rigid, if you please."

He smiles lopsidedly, a dimple appearing in the side of his cheek. It is all I have to remain stone-faced, to not grin myself.

"*Shall I compare thee to a summer's day?*"

"My patience grows thin, Alexander. I'm sure you didn't come here to spout poetry to me."

He slides the book back onto the shelf.

"Do you remember how Peter reacted that first night you were here?"

I fold my arms across my bust. "You mean how he ignored me completely? Flirted with Elizavetta?"

He turns back to me, one eyebrow arched. "Did this evening remind you of anything?"

I open my mouth to say no, to say that he had been perfectly kind and attentive all evening. But then I stop.

He ignored Charlotte. He flirted and fawned over me, but ignored her almost completely.

My expression must give me away because Alexander sighs.

"I'm so sorry, but I wanted you to see that this evening was not the victory you hoped it was."

I lick my lips slowly because my mouth has gone dry. "Peter's playing games again."

Alexander nods solemnly. A ball of silent fury builds inside me. How could I have been so stupid? Of course he wasn't genuinely interested in me. How could I have been so easily fooled? I replay every moment in my mind, our ride, the picnic he made for us. Had it all been a ruse? I square my shoulders and lift my chin. I'll have to redouble my efforts to catch his attention. Perhaps I gave in too quickly, or perhaps I needed to remain more aloof? Then another, much darker thought occurs to me.

My head snaps up. "Why are you telling me this?"

Alexander takes a step back, looking affronted.

"Peter is your friend; I am just a stranger from another country. So why do you tell me these things? Or are you more part of this game than you would like to admit?"

I swear I see him blush before he looks away.

"*It lies not in our power to love or hate, for will in us is overruled by fate. When two are stripped, long ere the course begin, we wish that one should love, the other win.*" His voice trembles on the last line, and it does not escape my notice.

I know the poem. Marlowe is one of my favorites. His verses of love and longing are deep and still, something I often allow myself to indulge in. This poem, in particular, resonates with me. I complete the last line.

"*Where both deliberate, the love is slight. Who ever loved, that loved not at first sight?*"

He turns back to me.

"If any were to remain here, as empress, I wish it to be you. Should Peter's heart fall to a beautiful face, he need look no further than what is right in front of him."

My heart skips in my chest painfully. I stare at him for a long moment, unsure what to say. He is a dark beauty. His gaze is fervent and almost excruciating to behold. Unlike the others at court, all golden hair and fair skin, he feels wild.

Dangerous, a soft voice whispers in the back of

my mind.

"If he marries you, then you can remain here, at court." He rakes a hand through his hair in a boyish gesture. "And I would have you stay, for purely selfish reasons. So that I might—from a distance—be allowed to behold you."

His words slice through me like a sword, sharp and quick. I know I cannot indulge this feeling I have—a feeling we seem to share. But there is something else, a deep longing that threatens to overwhelm me. I open my mouth to speak but the room spins, my stomach churning. I stumble back as my knees go weak. I feel myself fall, and his arms catch me as I collapse.

"Princess?" his voice calls out to me as if from a great distance. "Sophie?"

He sets me gently into a chair. I place my hand on his chest and open my eyes. The room has become unbearably hot, and I feel weak as a newborn kitten. Under my fingers, I feel his heart pound, strong and steady. I focus on the sensation, clutching it like a drowning man might clutch a rope. In that moment, he is my lifeline, the only thing tethering me to the earth.

"I need to get back to my room," I whisper hoarsely.

Without a word, he scoops me up, cradling me in his arms. I rest my head in the curve of his neck. His skin is cool compared to mine so I nuzzle against him, touching him everywhere I can find exposed flesh. I know I shouldn't touch him so, but the rational part of my mind is being burned away in a haze of fever.

I don't see the guard throw my door open, but I hear it. Alexander orders him to fetch the physician, lays me across the settee, and wipes my hair back from my face.

"Go," I order softly. "They can't find you here."

I hear him curse lightly under his breath and I feel a quick, nearly imperceptible kiss graze my forehead before he releases me and backs away. As soon as I'm sure he's gone, I call out to my mother, who rushes into the room. Seeing me, she screams for help. I roll off the lounge and spill onto the cool floor. A pain in my chest rises up and I cough, suddenly unable to catch my breath. When I look down, I see sprinkles of blood pooled on the floor under me. Then a thick, white fog fills the room. I try to swat it away with my hand, but it's no use. It consumes everything, and I feel my arms give out under me. The last thing I remember is wishing, that if I were about to die, that I could do it back in Alexander's arms.

Chapter TEN

The next hours are a frantic blur. I vaguely feel myself being taken to bed, the old, bearded physician tending to me with damp cloths and vials of grotesquely scented balms. I catch glimpses of Mother, of my ladies, and once, of Peter's concerned face. I doze in and out of consciousness often. Being awake is torture; my body is wracked with pain, as if on fire from the inside. Every piece of me hurts. I bite my lip against the suffering, for fear I will call out, and for fear of who I will call out for.

A cool, damp cloth lies across my forehead, and I hear the empress' voice like thunder.

"You stupid, naive woman. If the physician says he needs to bleed the girl, then he will bleed her. I will not allow your silly superstitions to cost Sophie her life."

I don't have to open my eyes to know she is speaking to my mother. Mother distrusts doctors in general, and especially disliked the practice of bleeding a patient. Her own mother was a healer, and she knows the risks of such a thing. Still, my blood is boiling; I can feel it. Letting him take some of that away is a mostly pleasant thought.

Someone sits next to me; the bed sinks down at my side. At first, I think it's my mother re-soaking my cloth. But when I manage to open my eyes, I see Empress Elizabeth's radiant face looking down at me worriedly.

"You are very ill, child. The physician is going to bleed you."

I nod just a bit, and it sends the room spinning. It's all I can do not to retch.

"He thinks, my dear, that you are close to death." She pauses. "But he does not know you."

She soaks the cloth and wipes my face gently.

"He doesn't know of your strength, of your courage. You remind me of myself in that way."

"Thank you," I manage weakly, earning me a smile.

"Your mother wants you confessed. She is off fetching a Lutheran priest."

With all the effort I can muster, I take her hand.

"No, fetch me Bishop Todorskey," I beg. The empress' smile widens at the mention of his name. He is a great man in her esteem, and some very distant part of my mind still clings to the need to please her. Though I have not yet begun the process of my conversion to the Orthodox Church, I know I will—if given the time—do whatever it takes to win her affection completely.

She sits back, propping herself among my pillows, and draws my head into her lap, stroking my hair and singing softly as the physician takes my arm and begins applying the leeches. The sound of her voice is like an angel in my head, and I allow myself to drift off to sleep.

The next time I am fully awake, my mother stands in the door, arguing with Count Lestocq. I can't quite make out their words but he leaves abruptly, and she turns her sour gaze upon me.

"You were moaning in your sleep last night; it made it quite unbearable for me. Please, in the future, suffer in silence like a true German." And with those cold words, she lifts her skirts and leaves the room.

Sometime later, the empress arrives, her large, green-and-gold gown swishing through the room as she sits beside me, once again taking my head in her lap.

As the physician comes to take more blood, she recounts the happenings of court.

"You should be proud. It's been five days since your first bleeding, and you are still with us. Growing stronger too, I think. Though your fever is still high. I've had to tell Peter he cannot come visit, of course, for his safety. His health has always been questionable. No reason to risk him contracting anything."

I groan, and she takes it for grief rather than pain at the procedure.

"Be still, little darling. Peter is occupying himself

well enough. Tomorrow, he is leaving for Moscow with Count Lestocq to see to some matters of state, and he is going hunting while he is gone. Of course, he wishes you were well enough to join him, but hopefully by the time he returns, you will be well again."

She goes on, promising to throw the most opulent and grand masked ball to celebrate my return to court. Then the physician, done with his duties, leaves us alone. She strokes the side of my face in a motherly gesture.

"And I will promise you this, if you survive, I will see to your marriage to my nephew immediately. Think of this sickness as a trial from God, to test you and perfect you for the coming days."

She kisses my forehead gently and slips out of the bed, tucking the blankets around me before she goes.

I want to ask her why she dares to visit me in this condition. Isn't she afraid she will become ill as well? But my mouth is too dry to form words and like a summer breeze, she's gone and my room is dark again.

That night, Sergei slips into my room, throwing my window open wide. I have to admit, the fresh, cold air feels wonderful against my hot skin.

He takes a seat in a high-backed chair beside my bed and reaches out to take my hand.

"How are you feeling?" he asks.

I lick my lips. Over his shoulder, he calls for someone to bring me water, for which I'm extremely grateful.

They bring in a large goblet, and he holds it to my mouth while I drink. I reach up to take it from him, but I'm shocked to see my own hand, pale white and skeletal.

"How long?" I manage weakly.

"Ten days," he says with a worried frown. "We were sure you were lost to us. What do you remember?"

Though everything else is hazy, I remember the moments before I'd been stricken, those minutes spent with Alexander in the library. If I had any blood left in my veins, I might have flushed.

"Not much. My maid delivered some milk because I was having trouble sleeping. I went for a walk, started feeling ill, and came back to my room. Then it's all very spotty."

He nods. "I don't believe you are ill at all. The physician and I have been discussing it at some length. We think you were poisoned."

I frown. Poisoned?

The milk.

"By whom?"

Sergei rubs the whiskers on the side of his face. He looks much older today than I remember. Perhaps it's stress.

"How old are you?" I ask boldly. He grins.

"I'm a ripe old twenty, Princess."

"You seem older."

He grins again. "You must be feeling better, to

insult me so."

I open my mouth to protest, but he stops me.

"I'm teasing. Please, keep still. I fear the physician has been over excited about your bleeding."

I settle back onto the pillows, allowing myself to relax.

"And Peter?" I ask finally. The smile falls from Sergei's face.

"Peter has been spending some time with Princess Charlotte. Though I hear she is growing quite frustrated with him constantly asking after you. He was quite upset that the empress wouldn't allow him to see you."

"Haven't you shared your suspicions with her? About the poisoning?"

He nods.

"Yes, and she agrees. Though she seems quite unwilling to accept that one of her own may be responsible."

"What do you mean?"

He arches one dark eyebrow and I realize that in a vague way, he reminds me of Alexander. They could, in fact, be brothers. They have the same strong, chiseled jaw, the same dark hair, and the same olive skin. The only difference is their eyes. Sergei's are darker green and brown, and full of intensity as he looks at me now.

"I mean to say the empress knows you aren't ill, but she thought that perhaps, in your absence, Peter's affection for you might grow. And she seems to be right."

Of course it is, I think miserably. Peter only wants what Peter can't have. Thankfully, I no longer need to worry over Peter's flighty attentions. I have the empress' promise of marriage. I just need to get well enough to make it happen.

"She has tasked me with finding the person behind the attack," he adds flatly.

I sip some more water.

"And you have your suspicions?"

"I do, but suspicions are worthless without evidence."

I frown.

Patting me on the legs, he forces a smile. "But none of that is your concern. Leave the matter to me, and I will do what needs to be done. Here, I have just the thing to occupy your mind."

With a large book in his hand, Sergei and I begin more Russian lessons. I'm grateful for something to keep my thoughts engaged, and I'm genuinely sorry when he finally puts the book down to leave.

"You rest, Princess. I'll be back tomorrow."

"Thank you. And Sergei," I say. He pauses, looking at me expectantly. "It means a great deal to me to have you. This is a... difficult place, and I think sometimes you are the only person I can truly count on."

Putting his hand to his heart, he bows. "You, my dear Sophie, can always rely on me. I am your true and devoted servant."

He smirks gently and bows again before leaving the room.

The wind blows through my window, making the sheer curtains dance in the streaming moonlight. I have only just begun to drift off when I hear my door creak open slowly.

Alexander peeks his head in. "Princess, are you well enough that I might speak to you for a moment?"

I know that it's late, far too late for visitors, and beyond that, having a young man alone with me in my room is beyond inappropriate. Still, he's looking at me with those green-gold eyes, and my resistance fails.

"Come in," I say, adjusting myself to sit up.

He takes the seat Sergei vacated, placing a vase of fresh flowers on my bedside table. The smell is fresh and reminds me of springtime. Lilacs and honeysuckle, two of my favorite blossoms.

"They are lovely, thank you," I offer weakly.

He smiles, dimples appearing in his chin and one cheek. "I've been so worried. I haven't dared visit you until now. I'm sorry for that."

I shake my head. "Don't be. I've been too unwell to see anyone."

"Peter says you are ill, but there are rumors floating around the palace..."

I take a shallow breath. "Yes, I believe I was poisoned."

His jaw twitches at my words.

"And who do you think to blame?"

I shrug. "There are many people who wish me gone from court. But the empress is aware, and she is keeping a much sharper eye on things now. I doubt someone would dare try again."

He lets out a deep breath, leaning forward.

"If I ever find out who did this, I swear to you, I will kill them with my own hands."

I take his hand. Its rash and unthinking, but I've missed him terribly—I didn't realize how much until this very moment. His skin is cool in my fingers, and I can feel his pulse speed up. I don't look up into his eyes—I don't dare—I just keep looking at our entwined fingers.

"Please don't do anything rash. My time at court would be too dark to bear without your presence."

I don't know why I let the words slip out. Perhaps it was simply because I'd been so close to death for so long that the idea of living another moment in anything but the truth made my heart ache. Or perhaps, it was the fever speaking, separating my heart from my rational mind.

Bending down, he kisses each of my fingers, and then the back of my hand. His lips are soft and warm with his breath. A chill shivers through me. Releasing me, he sits back, as if the gesture pains him, and he grimaces.

"I see someone has brought you reading material.

These lessons will be the death of you yet," he teases. Cracking a book, he begins reading to me, his voice deep and thick.

"Of man's first disobedience, and the fruit of that forbidden tree whose mortal taste brought death into the world, and all our woe, with loss of Eden..." he reads softly, his voice barely a whisper. *Paradise Lost* by Milton. Not nearly as poetic or romantic as Shakespeare, but soon, I feel my eyelids begin to droop. I only wake when he closes the book and the morning light is just beginning to glow through my window. He stands, and I grab his hand.

"Please, come read to me again tomorrow. This time something from Marlowe?"

He smiles and bends down, placing a quick, chaste kiss on my hand.

"As you wish, Princess."

Then he turns and creeps from my room.

I sleep a fair bit of the day away, waking only for my afternoon lesson with Sergei, who comments how rested and well I'm looking. While he reads the dry text, I sip warm broth. The physician has decided not to bleed me today—thank heavens. And I am feeling weak, but excited. I repeat the passage back to Sergei. I don't tell him about my visitor, or about the unexplainable push of heat through my veins at the very notion of seeing him again tonight. When we are done, before he leaves, I have to ask.

"Sergei, where is my mother? I haven't seen her

in days."

He frowns. "I didn't want to burden you with this while you are recovering, but your mother has been sent to Moscow. The empress thinks having her here is... unproductive for you."

He hesitates, and I can feel the lie in his words as he looks away.

"Please, be honest with me, Sergei. If I can't find truth in you, what hope do I have here?"

He faces me, his expression filled with guilt.

"The empress believes she may be spying for King Frederick. She has sent her away as punishment."

I suck in a sharp gasp. Part of me wants to rail in her defense, but there is a larger part that is relieved that she's gone.

"Don't worry yourself," he says, reaching out with his thumb and rubbing me between the eyes where my brow is furled so hard. "When you are well, you need only request her returned to court and she will be. The empress is a very forgiving woman."

I catch his hand in mine.

"Thank you, as always, Sergei."

He smiles. "For you, dear Sophie, I would rope the moon itself and drag it to your window."

I feel myself flush as I return his smile.

If Rina thinks it odd that I have her help me bathe and brush my hair only to go back to bed, she says nothing of it. She and Elizavetta seem absolutely ecstatic that I'm feeling well enough to move at all.

Though it takes both of them to lower me into the hot water and back out again, they chat merrily.

"They eat like pigs," Elizavetta tells me.

Rina adds, "The seamstress has had to repair several of the princess' corsets because she keeps them so tight that she bursts the strings when she dances."

They laugh and make absurd faces in imitation of the Saxon guests. But mostly they speak of Peter, of how he paced outside my door for days, sick with worry for me. I feel a roll of guilt wash through me, though I have no doubt they are exaggerating for my benefit, I also know that his concern was real.

As they help me back to bed, Rina places a small, pink cake next to my bed.

"It's your birthday," she reminds me. "I thought you might have lost track of time being so ill, but I wanted you to know we remembered."

"So did the empress," Elizavetta chimes in, bringing me a wooden box engraved with the image of a crown. I open it to find a breathtaking sapphire necklace inside. "She only wishes she could have given it herself."

"It's so lovely," I say, caressing it with my fingertips.

Elizavetta shrugs. "You don't turn sixteen every day, after all."

"And, there's one more. It's from General Salkov." Rina hands me a parchment-wrapped gift tied with red ribbon. I tear into it and find a lovely new bible inside. Opening the first page, I see it's in Russian.

The inscription reads,

For when you need counsel beyond my own. May you always be the light in dark places and the heart of the empire. Yours always, Sergei.

I clutch it to my chest, unable to hold back the raw emotions threatening to overwhelm me.

"Thank you both so much," I manage weakly. Rina hugs me tightly, and then pulls the blankets up over me.

Alexander comes again that night, with a fresh vase of flowers and a simple leather pouch. I pour the contents into my hand.

"Dirt?" I ask curiously.

"Soil from your homeland. I know how desperately you've missed being on German soil. Now you can carry it with you always."

I don't know what to say as I carefully pour the dirt back into the pouch. It's a piece of home, in this distant land. How much trouble had he gone to in order to get it? That he knows me so well, that this would be his gift, it fills my heart with joy. This simple pouch of dirt is worth more to me than all the rubies and diamonds in Russia.

"Thank you," I say sincerely. It doesn't seem like there are words enough to express my gratitude, so I just smile.

"Happy birthday, Princess," he offers meekly.

Alexander comes again the next night and the next and the next, sitting at my bedside, reading me tales and poems until I can almost feel the sun awakening from its slumber. And every night when he leaves, a sense of loss and dread fill me. I spend my days longing to see his face, and my nights staring into his eyes. He's always a gentleman, despite the very nature of the meetings, and never makes inappropriate advances, though a very deep, very reckless part of me wishes he would.

Weeks pass slowly, a languid, calm pace. The new moon comes and goes, and comes again.

By the time full night has fallen and my ladies and maids have long since retired for the evening, I sit in bed, thinking of how I can send Alexander away. I am to be Peter's wife, after all. How can I marry one man and long for another? It isn't fair. All the things I thought I wanted now sit within my grasp, and I can only think of my own selfish desires and of the one man who makes me question it all.

I should end these meetings, bury my feelings, and forget about him. I know that. I'm just not sure how.

My good intentions aside, the moment Alexander steps through my door, all those thoughts evaporate like morning frost.

Seeing me, he grins, bowing deeply.

"*Was this the face that launched a thousand ships,*

and burnt the topless towers if Ilium? Sweet Helen, make me immortal with a kiss."

His words, the words of my favorite poet spoken from his lips, soothe my troubled heart. Crossing the room to my bedside, he takes my hand, kissing it gently.

"Alexander, I must ask something of you," I begin softly.

His eyes flicker up, a glimmer of fear in them. I feel the same fear in my heart, the fear that tonight will be the night that I send him away, and even as I think it, I falter.

So I say the only thing I can think of.

"I have been in this bed for weeks, and I crave a change of scenery. Is there some place you could take me, some place where no one will see us? These walls feel too constricting."

Something else flickers in his eyes now, something I'm not familiar with.

Hope, perhaps? Or just surprise?

When he doesn't respond, I waver, feeling silly. Had I mistaken his kindness and concern, for something it was not? Surely, like Peter, he was a flirt by nature, but I was so confident that he felt the same as me, had I been mistaken?

"Of course," I mumble feebly, "I know it's quite inappropriate to ask such a thing of you. Please, don't think me ill-mannered—"

Before I can finish, he scoops me up, into his arms.

Chapter Eleven

We walk slowly through the outer chamber and into the hall, down the corridor and to an area I don't think I've ever seen. He carries me up a spiraling stone staircase that leads to a small door. He carefully pushes it open, exposing a small, abandoned chapel. There's one window adorned with stained glass in a riot of blues, greens, and reds. There's a long, red velvet bench and a small table.

"What is this place?" I ask softly as he sits me on the bench.

"They say it used to be Tsar Alexei's private sanctuary, a place he would come to speak to God before battle. It was never officially christened, but it was his secret place, removed from the old palace and brought here during construction."

He lights the candles that sit on large sconces, flooding the room with light, before taking a seat next to me.

"I come here sometimes when I need to clear my head," he admits. "It's my secret place."

"And you brought me here," I say, feeling both honored and touched.

He shrugs, not meeting my gaze.

"Now it's *our* secret place," he whispers.

I reach out, taking his chin in my fingertips and tilting his head up. There are so many things I want to say. Part of me is screaming that this is wrong, than I should leave now, but I can't. Because that part of my mind is being drowned out in a storm of other thoughts, the loudest being, *This is what you've waited all your life for, Sophie. Finally, you know what love feels like.*

"Alexander." I whisper his name like a solemn vow. My chest rises and falls in my simple sleeping gown. I wish I was prettier for him, clothed in the finest silk, my hair pulled up in perfect curls and tied with ribbon. But I know that I'm not. I'm pale, sickly, and thin after my ordeal. But looking into his eyes, I don't think he sees any of that. Because he is looking at me the way a man dying of thirst might look at a cask of water, as if his very life depends on bringing me to his lips. I know that being here with him is a terrible risk. I know I should tear myself out of this trance, but I can't. I'm lost in him.

And then he does the most dangerous, reckless thing he could have ever done.

He kisses me.

The moment our lips touch, the last fraying strands of my self-control snap and I reach up, clasping my hands behind his neck and pulling him against me. There's no reason, no judgment—only gentle waves of relief. I'm lost in the ocean of his embrace, drowning in him. I could live a hundred lifetimes inside his kiss, and it would never be enough. One single thought surfaces through the tide of emotions.

"Of the entire universe, I only wanted you," I whisper the words against his lips, a solemn pledge.

His hands slide up my back and into my hair, working it loose with his fingers until it falls in brown waves across my shoulders. I sigh against his mouth and he responds by pulling away just a bit, laying a kiss on the tip of my nose, my forehead, and beside my eye, before returning to my lips.

"You have ruined me," he whispers against my mouth, his voice thick with desire.

I can't help but laugh.

"And I would ruin you again," I say breathlessly.

He takes my face in one hand, the other running along my collarbone, brushing the hair back over my shoulder. "*Her lips suck forth my soul, see where it flies. Come, Helen, come, give me my soul again. Here I will dwell, for heaven is in these lips.*"

He leans forward, capturing my mouth with his, this time gently, reverently. He slides closer, his hand gliding down to the small of my back. A chill runs through me like nothing I've ever felt. It hums along my body like the strike of a piano key, music vibrating through me until it aches to contain it.

My head spins, the room around us falling away, or at least that's how it feels, until I hear Alexander's voice cut through me.

"Sophie," he says urgently. I open my eyes and realize it's not the room that's falling, but me. Only his strong arms locked around me keep me from sliding to the floor.

"Alexander?" I ask, unsure what's happening. The feel of his arms, the warmth of his kiss, it's all mixed and mingled in one strange, glorious blur of sensation.

He touches my head gently. "You're burning with fever," he says, wiping the hair from my face. "I need to get you back to your room."

I clutch his shirt. "No. Please, not yet. Just hold me for a while. Just hold me and whisper to me."

I trace my fingers along his lower lip and he sighs deeply before pulling me onto his lap, wrapping his arms around me, whispering my name over and over again.

"Please, sweet Sophie, you must be strong now. Be strong for the promise of spring, for the chance to feel the wet grass beneath your feet once more. Be strong for the hope of joy, for the hours we can share in each other's arms."

His words are paint, creating a masterpiece in my mind as I close my eyes. I can see it so clearly, us walking through the meadow, to the edge of the pond where the wild roses are in full bloom. He will take my hand, lay me down in the soft grass, and kiss me gently. Then, years later, he will put his hands to my swollen belly, a look of awe and joy radiating in his smile. I can see a tiny face, dark like his father's, resting nestled in my arms. I see our whole life stretched out before us.

And it's beautiful.

Then the dream shatters and I wake in my bed, the sun streaming through the window, and I'm alone. The pain is unbearable. I curl up my pillow and sob into it. I'm still crying when Rina arrives with the maid and my breakfast. She rushes to my side, stroking my hair.

"My lady, what is it? Are you unwell? Should I fetch the doctor?"

I shake my head, and she holds me while I cry.

"Oh, Rina, it's so awful."

"What is, my lady?"

I clutch her, wiping my tears on the sleeve of her gown.

"I never had a dream before. A beautiful dream. I was so happy..."

She strokes me gently, "It's the fever, my lady. It's playing tricks on your mind."

I shake my head because I can't tell her the truth. I'm in love with a man I cannot have. How cruel is fate that it would only show me the thing I want most, the thing I never knew I always wanted, only to snatch it from my grasp? Suddenly my marriage to Peter isn't a simple fact of life... it's the chains that bind me, the obstacle to my one true joy.

That's when I realize that I cannot be with Alexander. My duty is to my family and to do what I came here to do, I must let Alexander go. Being in love with him while being wed to another would be the most unimaginable torture. And if I had been well last evening, who knows how far things would have gone? Heaven knows I wanted him, and I felt that he wanted me as well. One reckless night, one unwise decision, could have cost me everything.

Everything I no longer want.

And how would it be fair to him? Standing so near to me, watching as I marry another, bear another man's children. It would be the worst kind of torment.

Finally, I sit up, wiping my eyes.

"Rina, fetch me some paper and a quill."

She obeys, her face soft but concerned.

I take them and hastily write my note before the courage of my conviction leaves me.

Stone walls do not a prison make, nor iron bars a cage; minds innocent and quiet take, that for an hermitage; if I have freedom in my love, and in my soul am free, angels alone that soar above, enjoy such liberty.

I fold the paper twice.

"Rina, I must ask something terribly important of you. Can you, telling no one, take this letter to Peter's man, Alexander? Please, it's terribly important and he will know what to do with it."

Rina nods. "Of course."

I take her arm. "Please, no one can know of this. Promise me."

She curtsies. "Of course my lady. You have my word."

"Good, go now. And send for Sergei. I need to speak to him urgently."

As soon as she's gone, I ring for my maids. They help me wash and dress. Soon, Elizavetta arrives to help me with my hair. Though I can still feel the flush of fever gripping me, being up and dressed helps improve my mood. The maids change the bedding and by the time Sergei arrives, I'm waiting to receive him in the outer chamber.

He bows deeply as he enters.

"Princess, I'm pleased to see you looking so well."

I nod and motion for him to sit.

"Elizavetta, please have some tea sent up."

She curtsies and leaves.

"Sergei, thank you for seeing me. I wish to begin my lessons as soon as possible. With Madame Groot."

He sits back, a coy smile playing across his lips.

"Really? You seemed so offended by the idea."

I nod. "I have decided that I must do whatever is required of me to possess the throne."

"You mean wed Peter?"

"They are one and the same, are they not?"

His expression becomes suspicious.

"Why do you want it?"

I rest my hands on my lap. I know what I should say—I should say that I'm madly in love with Peter and could bear no other. But that would be a lie and my heart isn't in it.

"My family is relying on me—on this marriage—to secure their lands and title. It is what is expected of me."

He shakes his head. "That's not a good enough reason."

I pause, gathering my thoughts before I speak.

"Because I cannot win. I cannot have what I truly desire—it is beyond my grasp. I realize that now. It's sad really, to think that until I came here, I had no other dreams, no other desires but what my family wanted for me. I discovered my own mind and heart too late." I steel myself, leaning forward. "Fate has offered me an opportunity. A crown in one hand and a husband in the other. Even if I were to throw all that away, it would still not get me what I want. It would only serve to hurt the people I care about. I would be sent back to Germany in disgrace, and my family would lose everything. There is no way to win, but there is certainly a way to lose. My choice, what little choice I have, is not to lose."

He frowns. "You are, as always, wise beyond your years, Princess. And, as always, you have my devotion. If it is the crown you want, the crown you shall have."

"And I would like our Russian lessons to be held in

the library from now on. Being out of bed and moving about will do me some good."

The maid arrives with a tray of tea and biscuits.

"For what it's worth," he says, taking a cup, "I think you are making the right decision."

I shrug, taking a cup as well.

"It's easy to make the right decisions in the light of day. It's at night, when I am alone with my thoughts, that my emotions betray me."

He lifts his cup, saluting me.

"True words. I will speak to Madame Groot today. If the physician thinks you well enough, you can begin your instruction with her tomorrow."

"Thank you, Sergei. And how long before Peter returns?"

"Three days. The empress has ridden off to join them. They will be back at court shortly."

"And Charlotte?"

"She and her brother went with Peter and his entourage to Moscow. Though word is they will not be returning with them. The empress finds the girl pious and dull." He laughs deeply. "And I quite agree. The Saxon princess will have to find a crown elsewhere."

That afternoon, I join Sergei in the library for my lesson, though I arrive a bit early. I search through the shelves of books until I come across a familiar volume.

Richard Lovelace. Pulling it from its shelf, I let it fall open in my hand, exposing a scrap of paper tucked into the pages. I take it carefully and have a seat.

My Divine Helen,
I feel great sorrow in your words, yet I cannot but hope you will have the courage to speak them to my person.
Please, meet me again as of last.
Yours always,
~Paris

I take the paper over to the lamp and light it aflame. Did I have the courage to speak to him again? I must find it within myself, I decide. He is due that much at least. Though part of me joys at the thought of seeing him again, another part cringes, knowing the pain my words will cause us both. I scribble a note of my own, replacing it in the book before returning it to the shelf.

Wait for me, sweet Paris. For I will come.
~Helen

Sergei arrives for my lesson, and I'm still quite distracted; it does not go unnoticed.

"I think that must be all for today," he says kindly. "You seem tired."

I shake my head.

"What did the doctor say?"

"He says your recovery is nothing short of a miracle and that he would recommend you keep in bed another week at least. But I assured him you would rest at the earliest sign of fatigue. So please, do not make a liar of me."

I smile up at him, grateful for his intervention. The idea of another week confined to bed, being bled every day, makes me want to cry.

"Of course, I will be quite vigilant."

He hands me the book. "Here, practice with this on your own between lessons. You'll pick it up faster this way."

I clutch the book to my chest.

He offers me his arm and leads me from the library. As we turn the corner, we nearly run into Alexander.

"Off in a hurry?" Sergei asks playfully.

Alexander rocks back on his heels, bowing to me. "No, of course not. Just, wiling away the time before Peter returns. Please excuse me, Princess."

I nod, not looking at him. As we pass, the urge to turn back is strong. Only Sergei's arm in mine gives me the strength to keep moving forward.

That night, I dismiss the maids before they help me undress.

"I'll do it myself, thank you," I say, and they scurry from the room. If my ladies think it strange, they say nothing. Elizavetta is working on her sewing, and Rina is reading a large tome. I allow myself the opportunity to doze for a bit, only to be awoken by the bells chiming eleven. I open my eyes to find Elizavetta long gone off to bed, but Rina still reading quietly, her long, yellow hair hanging loose around her shoulders.

"My lady," she asks, seeing me wake. "Are you ready for bed?"

I shake my head. "I have been feeling quite heavy hearted since yesterday. I think I'm going to the chapel for a bit, try to find some comfort."

She nods. Though her expression is placid, I see a flicker behind her eyes.

"Please, speak plainly Rina."

She pauses, closing her book and setting it aside.

"It's just that, I want you to know you can confide in me. I will guard your secrets as closely as my own, on my life I will." She takes a breath. "And I worry for you."

I motion for her to take a seat beside me.

"Yes, that is fair. You have always been so kind and honest. I do count you as a friend. I hope you realize that."

She nods.

"I have... something of a delicate matter to attend to this evening. I hope that once it's done, my mind and heart will be settled again."

"Does it have to do with Alexander? He asked after you often while you were ill. Always with the look in his eye of a man obsessed, a man deeply in love."

I tilt my head, unable to meet her in the eyes.

"Yes, it does. The heart is a... difficult thing to

manage. But I will put an end to it tonight. There can be no future for us, I see that very clearly."

She takes my hands in hers.

"I'm so sorry. I wish there was something I could do."

I wish I could send her in my place, have her deliver my words so at least I would be spared the pain of looking him in the eye. *This never should have gone so far*, I chastise myself.

"As do I. But it is my responsibility, and I will deal with it."

Rina smiles sadly. "Spoken like a true queen."

Rina's words don't hold much comfort as I walk down the deserted hallway toward the secret room, though having someone to speak with it about does lighten my burden.

I push the door open. Alexander is already there, waiting for me.

Chapter
TWELVE

As soon as I close the door behind me, he rushes over, catching me up in his arms and twirling me around before setting me back on my feet and leaning forward, kissing me deeply.

I know I should put a stop to it, but I can't bring myself to break away. Finally, I push back, gasping for breath.

"I was afraid you wouldn't come," he says, clutching his body against mine. "I was afraid you would stay away, and I would never get to touch you or kiss you again." His words are rushed, his time bordering on desperate. Carefully, slowly, I extract myself from his arms and step back.

"I'm so sorry, Alexander. This never should have happened. I have to marry Peter, you know that."

He frowns and steps forward. I know that if he touches me, my resolve will fly out the window like a bird and I will melt into him, so I step back again, holding my hands up.

"Sophie, please," he begs. "Don't do this, don't

push me away."

The air between us is so thick that you could slice through it with a sword. I can barely breathe through it.

"I cannot allow this. The idea of being with him, all the while wanting, wishing for you, is more than my heart can bear. The only solution is for us to forget each other, to put our feelings aside and do our duty," I reason with quaking words.

He reaches out, catching my hands before I can stop him.

"If I could, I would offer you my heart, my soul, and make that be enough. But I know it is not. I know that Peter is your destiny. You are going to be the most beautiful, clever, kind empress Russia has ever seen. And I want to be there for that. But I can't think about that now because today, in this moment, all I want is you. The thought of losing you cuts me to my very marrow."

I look away, even as he draws me closer. The war rages inside me, one part wanting nothing more than to kiss him until the sun rises, another part knowing why I can't.

He tilts my chin up gently.

"If you want to send me away, tell me only that you do not love me, and I will go. I will never speak your name again, never touch your hand. I will pretend that the loss of you hasn't killed me."

I sigh, my hard-fought resolve fading quickly.

"I could never say those words, because they would be the gravest lie. Of course I love you. I love you so much that I risk everything just to come to you tonight. If anyone knew—I would be ruined, sent away in a cloud of scorn. No one would ever have me, and I would bear the shame all my days."

He takes my face in his hands.

"I would have you, in shame or sin, I would have you in any way I could, in any way you could give yourself to me."

He kisses me again, and I know I've lost. Reaching up, I wrap my arms around his neck, holding him to me. He smiles against my lips.

"My sweet Helen, for you I would be Paris, and for your love, I would defy God himself and then return to you for a kiss."

"Peter and the empress will return in a few days. What will we do? Meeting like this… it's too dangerous," I say, unwilling to pull away again.

"Do you trust me?" he asks solemnly.

I nod. "I do."

"And do you love me?"

"With all my heart and my life, I do."

He kisses my hair.

"Then trust me. Give me a few days and by the time they return, I will have a plan. In the meantime, if you need me—"

"I always need you," I interrupt.

He grins.

"If you want to meet me…" I open my mouth to interrupt again, but he puts a finger against my lips, which I kiss. "Leave me a message in a book. John Wilmont's letters to his mistress."

I frown. "Am I to be your secret mistress?"

He shakes his head. "No, my love. I will be yours."

Sunday comes and my ladies walk me to confession. I haven't caught a glimpse of Alexander in nearly two days, and my heart aches for him. I know we agreed not to meet for a while, until he could come up with a solution to our problem, but takes all my willpower not to rush to him when the chapel doors open and I catch sight of him seated inside. My heart leaps to my throat as we pass him. I can feel the weight of his gaze on my back, though I dare not turn around. Bishop Todorskey approaches me, resplendent in his red-and-white robes. He reaches out and I offer him my hand, which he kisses chastely.

"Princess, I am so glad to see you are well. I admit that I was overjoyed when you requested me at your side during your illness."

I incline my head to him. "I have come to see that the differences in your faith and that of my father's is less one of doctrine and more one of… logistics."

He smiles humbly, leading me to prayer.

When I enter the confessional, my heart is heavy.

I know I should commit all my misdeeds to God, that I may be clean, but I also know that the Bishop is the empress' advisor, and I think, as with many here in court, that his loyalty must surely lie with her. So I speak vaguely, of missing the man I love, of looking forward to our future together. I never utter Peter's name once. A lie of omission, perhaps. The least of my sins.

I leave the confessional and take a seat across the chapel from Alexander. A quick glance tells me his eyes are closed, his head bowed. I follow suit, though my prayers today are far different from others in my life. Today I pray for strength, for the wisdom to know my own mind and heart, and for the courage to follow it.

We leave the chapel and I stop in the library, checking the book for any messages. It's empty, so I leave one of my own. Not seeing him has grown unbearable. How will I survive when I'm married, when I have to leave him behind for good? Or was he serious when he offered to be my mistress?

Without thy light, what light remains in me? Thou art my light; my way, my light is in thee. I live, I move, and but by thy beams I see.

I tuck my note away quickly and head for the parlor where I'm to meet my new instructor.

Madame Groot is not at all what I expected. Her

gown is slender, none of the large hip bustles the women wear these days, and low cut in the bust, while somehow still seeming modest. Her dark hair is curled in a tall stack upon her head, her face powdered and lips rouged.

I enter and she stands, curtsying.

"Princess Sophia, how lovely to finally meet you." She motions to the wine and bread set out on the table. "Would you care to join me for a bite?"

I almost laugh. What had I expected? A brazen French whore in net stockings and garish underdressing, I suppose. The woman in front of me is probably in her early thirties, and holds an easily sophisticated wit about her. With a gracious nod, I take a seat across from her.

"It's a pleasure to meet you as well," I offer.

She smiles coyly, handing me a glass of red wine. "I imagine you expected something more… exotic?"

I nearly choke on my beverage. She is, at least, direct.

"Yes, I suppose I did. This is all very new to me."

She nods and waves her hand. "Oh, yes, dear. Anyone looking at you could see that."

I frown.

"Oh, no, you mustn't take that as a criticism, it isn't meant as such. I only mean to say that you have a virtuous look about you. It's a good thing, truly."

I take a bite of bread, not sure how to begin. Thankfully, she does.

"Don't be nervous, dear. There's no reason to be. This is a safe place. Anything we discuss in this room remains in this room. I want you to feel comfortable here. All right?"

"I shall try," I say honestly.

"Good. Before we begin, I wonder, do you have any questions? Anything you are dying to know but never had the courage to ask?"

Her face is serene, absently amused by my obvious discomfort. I try to remember what little my mother had told me.

"Does it hurt?" I blurt out. Then, embarrassment floods over me, and I drop my voice to a whisper. "I've… I've heard it hurts."

She takes a drink. "Not terribly. There is a moment of discomfort the first time, but that is all. To be honest, if you are able to relax and allow yourself to get swept up in the moment, there should be no pain at all."

"Truly?" I'd heard the pain was nearly unbearable. My mother likened it to being run through with a blade.

"Truly. The act of love can be a very beautiful thing. It's not something to fear." She pauses. "Of course, often couples are so young and so nervous, they bungle the whole thing. That can be a different story. But that's why I'm here. I'm here to set you at ease, so you have no cause to panic."

I sit back. I can't help thinking of my ill-advised night with Alexander. Of course we had never gotten close to… but, I couldn't help but wonder what it would be like if we had.

"What did you think of just now?" she asks suddenly, drawing me from my thoughts.

"Oh, nothing."

She takes another drink.

"Oh dear, I know that expression. It's love. So, you are in love with the good prince?"

I shift in my seat, preparing some lie. But she cuts me off before I can say anything.

"No, not Peter, then," she says. My head jerks up. "It's fine, dear. Many young ladies fall in love with a man before the man they marry. There's no shame in it, so long as you didn't act on those feelings?"

I shake my head. "No, of course not."

"Good, because you should know they have a custom here at court. Before you can be married, the physician will check to confirm your virtue. That won't be an issue, I assume?"

I shake my head.

"I thought not. So, tell me, when you think of this young man, what happens to you, physically?"

I frown. "What do you mean?"

"I mean, do your hands shake? Does your heart race?"

I nod sheepishly.

"All good things, dear. Believe it or not, men feel those same things."

I nod again. I know she's right because I've seen

the pained look on Alexander's face, felt the quake in his touch. But I say nothing.

"The trick, my dear, is being able to excite those responses from your husband. Men are created differently than us, and thus they must be treated differently. While each is unique, there are some general things you can learn that will help."

I'm too stunned to speak as she stands, beckoning to the valet from the hall. He's older than the boy at my door, probably near to Sergei's age, though he seems younger by virtue of being clean-shaven. She seats him in the chair she vacated, whispering something in his ear. He relaxes instantly.

"This is Phillip. He has helped me with demonstrations before," she whispers lightly.

She holds up one gloved hand, sliding it off slowly. "Men are tactile by nature. They respond best by touch. So when you are alone, use a technique I call the subtle touch."

As she sets her glove on the table, her hand just barely grazes his arm, and I watch as his eyes dart to the area of contact.

"They are also visual creatures. But one must be careful to be subtle, exposing too much, too boldly, does no good."

She knocks the glove to the floor, and then lowers herself slowly to retrieve it. As she dips, I see the valet's eyes dart to her chest.

"You see?" she asks.

I nod, feeling as if I should be taking notes.

She dismisses the valet and returns to her seat. We spend the rest of the hour talking plainly about things I should expect and the subtly of flirtation.

"Every man is unique in terms of what sets him at ease. Can you think of something Peter enjoys?"

"He likes hunting," I offer, unsure if that's what she meant.

She nods. "Then he may very well be comfortable outdoors. But that, I think, is an advanced lesson." She smiles wryly, as if she's just told a joke only she understands. "What else?"

I wrack my brain.

"He likes military things," I remember.

She looks off in the distance.

"Yes, that's something you can work with."

"How?" I ask.

She sets down her cup of tea. "My first suggestion, have a gown made that greatly resembles a military uniform."

"Then what?" I ask nervously.

She begins a detailed plan of seduction. We discuss everything from flirting to how to take a man's clothes off without tangling him up in them. Half the time I'm blushing, the other half of the time, I'm laughing until my sides hurt as she relays some of her favorite stories.

"I hope this was helpful," she says kindly.

I have to admit, it really was. I feel different,

confident somehow, in a way I never have before.

"How many lessons shall we have?" I ask, finishing the last of my wine and feeling a bit light-headed.

"However many you feel you need. Though at least two more. We still need to discuss ways to help you get yourself with child," she says with a smile.

With Peter's child, she means. My heart sinks. Will Alexander love me still when I'm fat with another man's child? The thought is too awful and I push it aside, suddenly eager to leave the room.

No sooner am I in the hall than Sergei sweeps by, taking me by the arm abruptly. We stop in a small alcove, and he presses me against the wall gently.

"I know the truth," he says in hushed, but angry tone, a slip of paper clutched in his hand. For one awful moment, I think he's talking about Alexander.

"I know who poisoned you," he says, seeing my confusion.

"Oh," I mutter, relief flooding through me. "Who was it?"

He frowns, checking over his shoulders to make sure no one else is around.

"It was that bastard Bestuzhev. He and The Duke of Dresden plotted together. They knew that by eliminating you, the empress would have no choice but to choose Charlotte as Peter's bride."

I swallow the information, not nearly as surprised or as angry about it as I should be.

"Bestuzhev is her closest advisor. He can get to

me at any time, and next time, he will be sure to get it right," I say slowly, trying not to sound as afraid as I suddenly feel.

Sergei pulls me into his arms and crushes me in an embrace, which I return. He is firm and solid, the one and only thing I can truly rely on in this place. Pulling back, he takes me by the shoulders. "I swear that I will not let anything happen to you. The empress is on her way back now. As soon as she arrives, I will see her and present her with my evidence. He will be gone before he can even try to strike at you again."

I nod, and he releases me.

"For now, just go back to your rooms and try to stay calm. One more night and we can put all this behind us," he promises before bowing and briskly heading down the hall.

I turn toward my room, then change my mind and head to the secret room.

It's hours before Alexander arrives and when he does, I'm standing in front of the altar, collecting my thoughts. As soon as I hear the door open, I turn, standing straight and still as he enters.

"What's happened?" he asks, his voice wavering.

"Sergei found evidence of who tried to kill me; it was Bestuzhev," I say flatly.

Alexander's face flushes. "I'll kill him."

I hold up a hand. "No, you won't. You will let the empress and Sergei deal with it. I won't risk losing you over this. What's done is done, and besides," I walk toward him slowly, reaching out to touch his face, "if he hadn't done it, how would we ever have found each other?"

He grabs my hand. "You almost died."

I lift my head, my voice steady.

"And I would do it again. I would die a thousand times, if each time I could wake up to your face."

He turns away, shaking his head.

"Don't say that. Please."

"It's the truth," I say softly.

"That doesn't make it easier to hear."

I wrap my arms around my waist, holding myself. His tone is defeated. I sense that he, too, has realized the hopelessness of our situation.

"Peter and the empress will be back at court tomorrow. As soon as they arrive, Bestuzhev will be locked away and my official conversion ceremony will take place the following day. I expect the empress will make mine and Peter's betrothal official shortly after," I recite, as if it were a shopping list rather than life-changing events.

"And you will marry him?" Alexander asks, turning to look at me.

My heart sinks.

"Offer me another option," I challenge.

He nods, stepping forward, and takes my hands.

"I've written to my father. My family—we lack title but have wealth enough. He would support our marriage."

I'm shocked to hear it.

"Really? But my engagement to Peter…?"

"Isn't official. The possibility of it hasn't even reached his ears. All he knows is that you are a visiting princess, and that I have fallen quite madly in love with you."

"And my family?"

He frowns. "I do not know what King Fredrick's reaction will be, only that my father assures me that he will send whatever he can to help them along."

It's a gamble at best. Frederick may be so angered that he strips them of everything, or he may wash his hands of the matter entirely and not retaliate at all.

"What would I tell the empress?"

My mind whirls with the possibilities. The empress is fond enough of me; perhaps if I bring her the truth, that my heart lies with another, perhaps she will release me. And Sergei, sweet, kind Sergei, who has risked so much to be my defender here, what about him?

"I think the best thing would be if we left without telling anyone."

I rear back, shocked by the idea.

"You mean run away? You are suggesting that we run away together?"

He smirks. "Consider it eagerly vacating."

I sigh deeply, falling to my knees.

"I don't know if I can do this," I admit weakly.

He sits beside me, and I rest my head against his

shoulder.

"If you can't, or if you decide you don't want to, I just want you to know I won't be angry. I won't blame you and I won't ever, ever leave you." He takes my hand, our fingers entwining. "I love you. No matter what."

"There you go, offering to be my mistress again," I say, trying to feign humor in the dreadful situation.

"You say it as if it's a joke. But I am yours, in any way you will have me. I will be your mistress if I must, but I would rather be your husband."

I sit up, forcing myself to look at him. There's no trace of doubt that I love him. But did I love him enough to risk everything, my family, my own life if we're caught?

Yes. There's no doubt. It's reckless and selfish and for the life of me, I can't force myself to care. I need to be with him like I need air in my lungs. And I would risk all that and more for even the slightest chance that we might have a life together.

"This is insanity," I say with a laugh, my decision made.

His expression changes, and I watch as his eyes fill with joy as he realizes what I'm saying. Moving to his knees in front of me, he clutches my hand to his chest.

"Sophie, queen of my heart, will you marry me?"

Chapter Thirteen

I lunge forward, wrapping my arms around him and closing the distance between us.

"Yes, yes, of course I'll marry you."

He kisses me, urgently, passionately. Heat boils up inside me until I think I might burst into flames from it. He slips my gown down, just off my shoulder, and kisses the skin there, tracing the lines with his lips. I moan, unable to help myself. This is what Madame Groot was talking about before, about turning yourself over to the pleasure. I knew there would never be any pain with Alexander. He would wrap me in his arms and drive away the fear until this was all that remained—the raw, driving need.

He slides one hand up my leg, under my gown, and I'm barely able to regain my wits long enough to stop him.

"Wait," I whisper.

He nods, burying his face in my hair, panting heavily. Drawing back, he cups my face in his hand.

"Soon, we will be married and there will be no

more waiting."

I turn my chin, kissing his palm.

"I long for that day," I say honestly, curling up in his arms.

I don't realize I've fallen asleep until the faint rings of the church bells rouse me. I count the chimes.

Eight. No, nine!

I jerk myself upright. Beside me, Alexander stirs.

"What is it?"

I leap to my feet. "It's nine. The empress will be here any time." I frantically tug at my gown, which is rumpled beyond salvage. "Oh no, my ladies will see I've not been to my bed this evening. Oh, the maids will talk—"

He stands, wrapping his arms around me and kissing my neck.

"Calm down. I'll leave first. You wait a few minutes, and then follow me out. Go straight to your room, and if anyone sees you, tell them you walked the halls all night, that you were too excited to sleep." In one smooth motion, he grabs my hips and spins me to face him. "Sophie, this only works if we get out of here before the official betrothal. We need to be careful, especially now that Peter is returning. If he thinks for a moment that you are slipping from his grasp…"

He lets that hang between us. The fact is Peter is so volatile, anything could happen.

"I'll leave you a letter in the book, so you know where and when to meet me. Be ready. By this time next week, we will be safely in Stockholm, and happily married." He kisses me quickly and leaves. I take a few minutes to smooth my gown and adjust my hair before following.

I manage to make it back to my room without being seen by anyone but the servants, a small miracle. But when I open the door to my rooms, what I see nearly makes me tumble. There, in a heavy, red gown, is my mother. She holds her arms out for me.

"Ah, my daughter. So good to see you well," she says, her voice high and thin. I glance over to Rina, who is standing by my door.

"My lady, back from your walk so soon?" she says gently. "Would you like a cup of tea?"

I nod, silently thanking her with my eyes. As soon as I walk over, she bends down, whispering, "I tossed your blankets about before the maids came."

"Thank you," I mutter again.

"Mother," I say, turning to face her. "What brings you back to court? The empress told me you'd been sent away. Are you back to spy for King Fredrick some more?"

She flicks her hand as if it was nothing rather than treason—an offence the empress could have her put to death for.

"The empress has been kind enough to request my presence at your official betrothal."

I force a smile but say nothing.

"She's sent for your little brother as well, but your

father has refused to allow him to come. He says the boy is unwell; I think he just doesn't want to be separated from his precious heir."

Her tone is curt and condescending, and it immediately makes me angry. Any concern I may have had over her well-being once I fled court was replaced by coldness. I point to her trunk on the floor. No doubt, it's full of new gowns and jewels purchased with her treasonous money from the Prussian King.

"You needn't bother unpacking," I tell her flatly. "As soon as the engagement is formalized, your presence here will no longer be required."

She looks at me, her mouth falling into a stunned oh.

"Well, your time in Russia certainly hasn't improved your manners, now has it?" She straightens her back, looking affronted. "Still, I am your mother and I will remain—"

"You will go as I tell you to. Your being here upsets the empress, and it upsets me. Go back to Prussia and do not return."

I motion for Rina.

"Rina, this gown is far too bland to welcome Peter home in. Please, come and help me change." I keep my voice calm, though anger is filling me. Mother's presence isn't simple a nuisance, but it will be an unwelcome complication to my plans. I want her safely away before I flee with Alexander, far from the rage I'm sure the empress will be feeling.

Rina helps me change in the privacy of my own room.

"Thank you so much," I say softly once we're alone.

She smirks. "Do I dare ask what kept you from your bed last night?"

I shrug, determined not to let her see my flush. "I was too anxious to sleep, so I went for a walk. I ended up in the library and fell asleep reading there. It was silly," I lie smoothly. Much as I was growing to love Rina, I had no desire to put her in the middle of this business. Plus, that way when I'm found missing and they question her about it, her ignorance will be genuine.

No, the only person I will truly miss is dear, sweet Sergei. My friend and ally. I hate knowing the trouble my departure will cause. But he will understand, as surely as anyone, why I could not stay. Once I'm safely in Sweden, I will send him a letter with my apologies.

Once I'm dressed, my ladies, my mother, and I retire to the grand rotunda, to wait for word of the empress' return. When we arrive, I see Sergei and Alexander chatting near the door. Both of my handsome men are looking relaxed and jovial, though I know each of them well enough to read their subtle tensions. Alexander clutches the lapel of his dark brown jacket and Sergei's jaw is tight even as he speaks, betraying their true emotions.

I sit with my ladies and strike up a game of cards. Soon, the trumpets blare and the valet announces the empress has arrived. We dutifully file out into the courtyard. The snow has melted away since I've been ill, replaced by lush green grass and fresh blossoms in the flowerbeds. Red-and-gold flags are driven into the ground, creating a pathway to the door. We take our places in line and I can't help but sneak a glance at Alexander, who stands across from me. Trumpets ring out again as the empress, never one to ride in a carriage, strides up on the back of her tall, black stallion and dismounts. Her riding habit is the same as a military officer's, only in deep blue and gold rather than the military-issue red. She pulls the gloves from her fingers and walks up the procession line, each of us bow or curtsy deeply as she passes.

I see Sergei break the line and follow her inside, no doubt wanting to speak with her immediately. The carriage pulls up next, and Count Lestocq and Chancellor Bestuzhev step out in all their finery. Lestocq is wearing a long, sky blue Caftan with lace and silver embroidery, and Bestuzhev is trailing behind him in flowing robes of gold. Neither of them looks happy as they approach the palace. Three horses arrive next, one carrying a breathless, disheveled-looking Peter, one carrying Mikhail, and one carrying a young man I don't recognize. Peter catches sight of me in the crowd and practically leaps from his horse. Rushing over to me, he lifts me by the waist and spins me high into the air.

"My lovely Sophie, I am so glad to see you well."

"And I am glad to see you safely returned," I reply, unable to muster any enthusiasm at all.

"Have you heard the news? My aunt has finally sent that dreadful Saxon and her lot back to Austria."

I nod, letting him lead me to the door. "I believe I had heard something about that," I say.

Peter pauses to clasp hands with Alexander.

"My friend, my brother. I'm so glad to be back in your company," Peter greets him warmly.

Alexander smiles. "The palace wasn't the same without you. How went the hunt?"

Peter ushers us all inside.

"Unsuccessful, if you must know. Dreadfully dull, Moscow. Not a stag to be found. Though, the drinking was vastly improved."

Peter turns to me, "And you, My Princess. Last I heard, you were at the very cusp of death. A miracle, I think? Just further proof that even God himself wants to see you become my wife."

"It must be so," I say without inflection.

A thundering crash draws my eyes up from the floor. Peter and Alexander exchange a look and rush toward the sound, with me not far behind. We turn the corner to find two guards grappling with the chancellor.

"Your Majesty, please. Forgive me. I was thinking only of you and the good of your kingdom!"

"Take him to the dungeon," the empress yells, her face flushed with rage.

Peter steps into the room, Alexander at his back.

"Aunt? What has happened?"

She spares a glance at Sergei, who answers for her.

"Evidence was found that implicates the chancellor in a plot to kill Sophie."

The empress smoothes her hand down her stomach.

"It seems it was not a common illness that almost took our darling princess, but the wicked scheming of men. Bestuzhev had her poisoned in hopes of seeing the alliance with Prussia fail."

Peter's eyes widen and without another word, he storms from the room. Alexander follows him. I wish I could count on Alexander to cool Peter's rage, but I know that he is harboring his own desire to see the chancellor burn for what he's done.

The empress looks at me.

"I'm sorry, dear, for what harm has befallen you while in my care."

I bow my head. "These things were not your doing, Empress. I know that. I know you have affection for me and would never wish me any harm."

Crossing the room, she takes my hands.

"Sweet, strong, brave girl. You remind me so much of myself at your age. Clever beyond expectation and levelheaded. You are exactly what I would have wished for in a child of my own, had I been so blessed."

She kisses my forehead gently and steps back.

"I hear you are ready to go ahead with the conversion?"

I nod again. "Yes. I only waited for your return, that you might stand as a witness for me."

She looks genuinely touched at my request. "Of course I will."

I move to leave, but one other thought strikes me. "One last thing, Your Majesty."

She looks at me expectantly.

"My mother—I appreciate your forgiveness for her misdeeds and for allowing her back to court. But I think it best if she leaves. Immediately."

The expression of surprise on the empress' face is sincere.

"You do not wish to have your mother here for your wedding?"

I square my shoulders, and answer in my best, official tone.

"She has disgraced herself, and by extension, me. I do not trust her not to repeat her mistakes and, to be frank, she has never been a true mother to me. I often wonder if she feels any affection for me at all."

I watch as the empress' countenance changes, softening at my words.

"I will see her sent away tomorrow, immediately after the ceremony. And then, the day after, we will make the official announcement of your engagement to Peter. We will have the grandest celebration this palace has seen in years."

A lump forms in my throat.

"So soon? Surely, you will need time to prepare such an event."

"Nonsense. I have been preparing this for months, only your illness prevented it happening weeks ago."

I smile weakly and curtsy, turning to leave.

"Wait," she calls after me. "I have some matters of state to discuss, and I would like you to stay and witness. Someday, you may have to handle such things—lord knows Peter has no stomach for it—so stay. Listen and learn."

At her insistence, I take a seat, but I only half pay attention. Everything seems to be shrinking around me, the very walls closing in. It's all I can do to keep breathing steadily, to keep my hands folded gently instead of curled into nervous fists.

Sometime later, the empress finally releases me and I'm all too grateful. I practically run down the hall to the stairs leading to the dungeon. I want to make sure Peter hasn't done something he will regret. I'm halfway down when I hear the screaming, and I freeze. Footsteps rush toward me and I know I should move, but I cannot.

Alexander's face rounds the corner, speckled with blood.

I rush to him, taking his face in my hands.

"Are you all right?"

He grabs my hands and holds them to his chest.

"I'm fine," he whispers. "It's not my blood."

Looking back over his shoulder quickly, he urges me back up the stairs. As soon as we are out of the hall, he stops into a small alcove and presses his back against the wall, wiping his face in his hands.

"What has Peter done?" I ask, my heart racing. "Is the chancellor dead?"

Alexander closes his eyes, shaking his head.

"No, it's so much worse than that. I thought at first he was just going to beat the man—God knows I've been longing to do that myself—but he..." His eyes fly open, and he looks at me. "He started muttering about Bestuzhev trying to steal you away from him, how you belonged to him, and how he had to be punished."

I swallow, trying to process what he's saying.

"He was a man possessed," Alexander whispers finally. "He took a knife and began slicing him. Not deep enough to kill, but there was so much blood."

"I did not know Peter's feeling for me ran so deep," I admit softly, still stunned but unable to doubt his words.

He licks his lips. "I don't think it was that. I think that Peter sees you as his possession. You *belong* to him, that's what he kept saying. It was the kind of rage he used to express when he thought someone had stolen one of his toys. Not love, but obsession."

And if he ever found out about Alexander and me, that rage would escalate a hundred fold. He would kill us both, I realize. Suddenly, the idea of running away with Alexander seems impossible, far too great a risk. The empress might someday forgive me for such a betrayal, but Peter would not. He would chase me to the ends of the earth to see me punished. I turn my back to Alexander.

"This changes nothing," he whispers.

I don't look back at him.

"This changes everything," I say softly.

I hear him take a step and stop as another set of heavy boots stomps out of the hall.

"Sophie," Peter coos softly, approaching me.

I blink back the tears threatening to spill from my eyes and turn to face him. He holds his bloodied hands out to me, and I force myself to take them.

"The chancellor has been severely punished for his crimes. I assure you that he, and anyone else who thinks to prevent our union, will think twice before ever threatening you again."

I can't speak so I just nod vigorously and try not to look as shaken as I feel. Leaning forward, he presses his lips against mine and my stomach heaves. I can taste the bitter, salty blood on his lips and fight down a retch. Releasing me, he quickly jerks his head to Alexander, who follows him off down the hall, only briefly looking back at me. As soon as they are gone from sight, I turn and head down the stairs. I need to make sure Bestuzhev is still alive, that a man hasn't died for Peter's rage.

As soon as I'm at the bottom, I see the cell at the

end of the hall is open and I slip inside. The smell around me is thick enough to choke on, the stench of sweat and urine and worse things. Bestuzhev hangs from shackles dangling from the stone ceiling. His clothes have been mostly stripped off. He manages to lift his head weakly. Ribbons of blood and flesh hang from his face, chest, and arms.

"Come to finish me off?" he asks, his voice hoarse and low. I take a step back, calling to the guards.

"Fetch the physician. Quickly. And you, unshackle him and help me lay him down."

The guards exchange a confused look before shrugging and obeying.

Once he's on the ground, I roll him onto this back, examining the wounds. Alexander was right, they aren't deep enough to kill, more the shallow wound a hunter might use to skin an animal, removing the flesh but preserving the meat. When I look down at him now, that's what I see, meat. I take what's left of his clothes and rip them into pieces.

"Fetch me some water and some brandy. Quickly," I demand, sending the guard scurrying. He's back in a hurry, a bowl of water in one hand and a bottle of brandy on the other.

Carefully, I soak scraps of fabric in the water.

"I'm sorry, but this is going to hurt," I say to the chancellor, who is watching me through his one unswollen eye. I quickly pour the brandy over the cuts, making him cry out and arch his back. Then I begin laying the wet cloths across the wounds until the doctor arrives. He takes over, carefully stitching each cut with thick thread. The chancellor finally loses consciousness, a small blessing. When I finally climb the stairs again, the physician has gone and I've left orders for the guards to see that he received food and water as soon as he woke. It was the best I could do for the man who tried to kill me. And I genuinely hoped it was enough. I had his blood on my hands now, quite literally.

I walked to my room, unaware of the eyes staring at me as I passed. I was in a daze, shocked and confused. When I get to my room, I have the maids bring water and I begin washing myself. I'm still scrubbing the blood from my hands when Sergei arrives.

"I was worried about you," he offers gently, as if sensing my fragile state. I can feel the tears running down my face as I turn to look at him. He has a book in hand, which he sets on the table. Coming up behind me, he wraps his arms around me and takes the soap from my hands. I lean forward, grasping the cabinet, and let the tears flow while he washes my hands and arms. I'm aware of him at my back, of the strong, musky, pine scent of him. I feel his warm breath on my neck as he lathers his hands and rubs them along my own. Something about it makes me want to fall into him, to let him hold me and protect me until the awful memories are driven from my mind. But I'm too numb for that, so I just let him wash away the blood and then dry me with a soft towel.

"I'll call your maids to help you with your gown," he whispers against my ear.

"No," I manage. "Not yet."

He steps back, releasing me, and takes a seat.

"You know what Peter did?" I ask.

He nods. "The whole palace knows what Peter did. He seemed to take great pride in it, telling anyone who would listen. The empress was furious, of course, but what could she say?"

"I went down to see for myself. It was just awful," I say, trying to keep my voice from quaking.

"The whole palace knows what you did as well, Princess. The guards said you were like an angel, to try to save the man who tried to kill you. Peter has won their fear this day, but you have won their hearts."

I frown. "It wasn't some political strategy. That man almost died because of me."

"You almost died as well," he reminds me.

I shake my head. "And he should be punished for that. But what Peter did…"

I don't finish the thought.

"Peter wanted to prove a point, not just to you, but to everyone. He wanted people to know what he was capable of. He thinks that to rule, people must fear him. He doesn't have their respect. Most people think he's too feebleminded and drunk to be trusted with any matters of real importance, and he doesn't want their love. Fear is all that's left for him."

He lowers his chin, looking at me strangely, "But today, you have won both of the things he does not possess."

I throw my hands up.

"Why does everything have to be some ploy? Some desperate grab for power?"

He sits back, his tone amused. "Because this is Russian Court."

I sigh heavily.

"I need to rest, thank you for your concern, but I'm fine, as you can see."

He snickers. "As you say."

He stands, picking up the book he'd brought.

"Here, Peter's man asked me to bring this to you. He said you mentioned wanting to read it, but he'd taken it from the library."

I take the book.

"Thank you. Please send my excuses to the empress. I'm afraid I don't feel well enough to come down to dinner tonight. Please have something sent up."

He bows and leaves. When he's gone, I open the book and find the hidden note.

Thou art my way; I wander if thou fly.
Thou art my light; if hid, how blind am I?
Thou art my life; if thou withdraw, I die.

I crumple the paper to my chest, it's meaning clear. *Nothing has changed*, he said. But something has changed. I see now that I will not survive here. I will not survive Peter, politics, or a life without love. Running away with Alexander means more than just being with the man I choose, it means my very survival. We must run, as far and as fast as our legs will carry us, and pray it is far enough.

Chapter FOURTEEN

I don't sleep much that night. I keep dreaming that I've gone to meet Alexander, only when I arrive, Peter has cut him to pieces and I see only his dead eyes staring up at me. When the maid comes in with breakfast, I'm sitting up in bed, hugging my knees, my face puffy from crying.

Rina and Elizavetta help me bathe and dress, all the while talking about how the servants were gossiping, not just about what Peter had done to the man who tried to kill me, but how I'd been so merciful and forgiving.

Rina encourages me to eat, a few bites of honeyed biscuit and a sip of tea, before finally sending for some vodka to calm my nerves. Elizavetta hands me a small glass, taking one for herself as well. It's bitter and strong, but I feel its affect immediately. My belly warms and my muscles relax. I smile despite myself, and she laughs, refilling my glass, which I quickly empty again.

"The ceremony won't be too bad," she assures me,

brushing my hair and pinning it up.

I nod, my neck beginning to feel like jelly. Elizavetta begins reading from the scriptures. I listen in a haze of warm relaxation until Sergei and my mother arrive.

"Are you all right?" Mother demands, looking at me with narrowed eyes.

Rina intervenes in my behalf.

"The princess has been fasting in preparation for the ceremony. She's a little weak."

I blink, widely, nodding in agreement. Mother looks satisfied.

"I've had a special gown made for you to wear today. I'm going to go fetch it."

"That sounds lovely, thank you," I manage. As soon as she leaves, I burst into laughter, joined by my ladies.

Sergei grins wildly, picking up my empty glass and sniffing it.

"You are completely drunk, aren't you?"

I shake my head. "No, just a bit I think."

He sits beside me, looking completely pleased.

"Well, no more of that until after the ceremony, all right?"

I nod, and Rina takes the glass away.

"Now, you will need to recite your vows. Do you have them memorized?"

I take a deep breath, trying to focus. The book he'd given me to study had been more helpful than perhaps he imagined. I recite the oath in perfect Russian.

He claps. "Well done. The empress will be pleased."

I stand and take a deep bow, nearly tipping forward, bringing in another round of uproarious laughter. Sergei catches me and sits me back down.

"All right, settle yourself before your mother returns. Why, today of all days, do you choose to begin your life as a drunkard?"

I lean forward, my elbows on my knees, holding my face in my hands. Sergei is so ruggedly handsome, with his dark, deep-set eyes and square jaw. Even the faint beard running along his jaw is so perfectly groomed that I can't help but wonder what it would feel like if I kissed him.

"You're very handsome when you are chastising me," I say with a sigh.

He sits back, a grin spreading across his face. "Then you will find me handsome quite often, I suppose."

I scoot closer to him, reaching out with my fingers to touch the side of his face. He captures my hand and kisses it quickly.

"As adorable as you are when you're inebriated, I need you to focus right now. Can you do that for me?"

I withdraw my hand and sit up, shaking off the stupor as best I can.

He sits back, pulling a long, blue box from his jacket and handing it to me.

"A gift from the empress."

I open the box to expose two snowflake-shaped pearl pendants and a large, gold-and-silver brooch with a huge emerald set in the center. All three are so lovely that it momentarily takes my breath away.

"Please send my thanks," I manage finally. "They are lovely."

"She wishes one other thing. You could be baptized by your true name, of course. But it is often custom to choose a new name, as a way to renounce all ties to your previous life."

I nod. I'd been aware of it but hadn't given it much thought.

"Her majesty asks if you would consider taking the name Catherine, after her own blessed mother."

I swallow. It makes no difference now. The conversion, the ceremony, all of it is for show. Something I am expected to do. I would cancel the thing altogether if not for my desire to keep Peter firmly in the dark about my intentions till the very last possible moment.

"Yes, I would be honored, of course."

When Mother returns, Sergei bows and takes his leave, giving me one firm glance before he goes.

Mother lays the gown across the lounge. It's similar to hers, heavy, scarlet taffeta with silver thread along every seam. Only where my mother's gown is inset with diamonds like tiny stars, mine is simple, a slender, silver vine along the bodice it's only embroidery.

"If I may make a suggestion," she offers, clasping her hands to her chest.

I nod.

"Consider wearing your hair down, something simple and stark. You are pale from the fasting and between the complexion, your dark hair, and bright blue eyes, the effect will be one of the utmost elegance."

Her tone is light, almost loving. But somehow, it isn't enough for me to want her to stay. Perhaps there has been too much coldness between us for me to allow her into my heart now. Or perhaps, my time at court has left me jaded.

"I will; thank you."

She curtsies—something she's never done in her life—and leaves quietly.

"Maybe she's drunk too?" Elizavetta offers, and the laughing begins again.

We dress and prepare to head to St. Peter's Cathedral, where the ceremony will take place. It's a brief walk from the palace, but the empress insists we take a carriage instead. The pins and brooch that the empress gave me are my only finery; I've left everything else behind. My hair hangs straight, cascading around my exposed shoulders, only a simple white ribbon holding it back off my face. I've put on no powder or rouge, only a bit of red wine to stain my lips. The effect, as Mother had predicted, is a bold one. As I walk into the chapel, I hear the rush of whispers around me, sighs and comments on my grace and beauty. I try to tune it all out and focus ahead of me, where the bishop awaits. From the corner of my eye, I see Alexander, but I don't look at him fully. Beside him is Peter, who frowns and whispers to Mikhail, and beside them the empress, who has tears in her eyes as she looks down at me from her seat in the balcony.

I walk slowly, keeping in step with the choir as they sing softly. Mother follows me, taking a seat in the crowded chapel as I reach the thick, white pillow and kneel. Over my head, the bishop recites a prayer and then begins anointing me with sacred oil. I close my eyes as he touches my forehead, both eyes, my neck, throat, and finally the backs and palms of each hand, consecrating them with oil as he prays.

Finally, the time comes. I raise my eyes skyward and in as loud, and strong a voice as I can muster, I recite my vows, the creed of my new faith, in flawless Russian, sending another ripple of awed whispers through the crowd.

The bishop pronounces my new name, Catherine, and the crowd cheers. He takes my hand and helps me to my feet, offering me to the masses as the newest member of God's true church. I keep my eyes fixed ahead of me, not reacting at all to the chaos erupting around me.

I'm ushered back to my room to dress for the feast. By the time I arrive, my head is pounding and my knees feel weak. As I'm changing, another box arrives from the empress, this one delivered by her own valet.

I open it to expose a stunning diamond necklace and matching brooch, both of which I put on for the banquet, along with the tiara Peter had given me. I plan to leave them when I go, of course, but it seems a shame not to wear them while I still can.

My ladies escort me to the feast. My stomach is rolling so badly that I can barely eat, and I'm glad when we retire to the ballroom for dancing and drinks. As soon as the maids set out the wine, I grab a glass, draining it quickly.

The empress, in her wide, lavish, silver gown, crosses the floor to speak with me. I curtsy.

"Your Majesty."

She smiles, fanning herself with a small, silk fan that matches her gown.

"My darling, you were stunning today, truly stunning. I knew I made the right decision bringing you here." She pauses, taking a glass of wine herself and leans forward. "And thank you for your kindness to the chancellor. He is a man with flaws, to be sure, but he is dear to me. I would hate to think what might have become of him had you not intervened."

"Yes, Your Majesty."

She flitters off into the crowd, looking for someone to dance with and finding Sergei looking roguishly handsome in his simple, well-fitted suit. Peter approaches me, his men close behind, and offers me his hand.

"May I have this dance, Catherine?"

I nod and curtsy before taking his hand and following him onto the dance floor.

"You looked lovely today. I don't know if I mentioned."

"Thank you."

"But I was a bit disturbed when news of your actions reached me. Is it true you took mercy on the man who tried to kill you?"

I swallow at the accusation in his voice. I'd never been afraid of Peter before, but after seeing what he'd done…

"Yes, my lord. If only for the sake of your aunt. She cares for him deeply."

His rebuttal is sharp, and I can't help but flinch.

"You need to concern yourself less with what pleases my aunt and more with what pleases me."

I try to keep the mood as light as I can.

"Of course, you're right. I'm sorry if I upset you."

"You undermined me."

"It was not my intent, I assure you. It was," I swallow again, "so kind of you to defend me in such a way. I only helped him in order to spare you your aunt's wrath if he should have died."

He takes my hand and grasps it so tightly it hurts.

"Let me worry about the empress."

I smile and let him spin me.

"Of course."

The music ends and he storms off the dance floor, leaving me standing there. As seems always the case,

Sergei comes to my rescue, taking my hand as another dance strikes up.

"Are you all right?" he asks as we move.

I shake my head. "Peter is cross with me about Bestuzhev. He thinks I undermined him."

Sergei says, "And now he's drinking. Not a great combination."

We draw close, and then back away, as the dance demands.

"But don't worry. I've had a little something slipped into his wine. Soon enough, he'll be fast asleep and he'll remain that way until morning."

I doubt there's anything else he could have said that would have brought such a smile to my lips. Just then, I hear a crash as Peter stumbles, dropping his glass of wine and falling into Alexander's arms, snoring loudly. I laugh loudly before I can stop myself, bringing a hand to my mouth to try and disguise it as a cough. Sergei smiles and spins me again.

"Thank you, Sergei. Thank you so much," I say, grinning widely as his men pick Peter up and head off to deliver him to his room. "I feel as though I'm forever thanking you."

He shrugs. "Then stop thanking me until you can find a more creative way to do it."

I cock my head, unsure if he's flirting with me. The devilish grin on his face suggests he is. When the dance ends, I excuse myself to the empress' table. She's sitting, surrounded by men as always, drinking wine from a golden cup.

I curtsy.

"Your Majesty, please don't think me rude, but I'm quite exhausted from the day. I think I should retire for the evening."

She smiles, waving me off with her hand.

"Of course, dear. Tomorrow is a big day after all."

I nod and curtsy again, excusing myself back to my room. Before I leave, Rina corners me.

"My lady, would you like us to come help you ready for bed?"

I shake my head.

"No, you and Elizavetta stay and enjoy the evening. The maids will help me."

She dips into a curtsy. "Of course. Have a good night."

"You as well," I offer, watching her walk away. I wish I could hug her, tell her that I might never see her again, and thank her for being such a good and kind friend. But I know that's impossible. So I leave, walking down the corridor until the last of the music dies away, replaced by stillness. A hand reaches out from a dark alcove and grabs me, pulling me inside. I almost cry out, but Alexander gently covers my mouth, shushing me.

I pull his hand away.

"What are you doing? Someone will see," I demand, my voice tight but soft.

He shakes his head. "Peter's passed out in his bed,

and everyone else is at the dance."

He pulls me close and steals a kiss that makes my stomach tighten, warmth spreading through me.

"Peter tells me that they are announcing the engagement tomorrow?" he asks.

I nod. "The empress doesn't want to wait."

He takes my face in his hands.

"Then we must leave tonight. Are you ready?"

"I've never been more ready for anything," I say honestly.

He peeks over his shoulder, making sure no one is around.

"There's a boat waiting for us at the wharf. Meet me at the stables at midnight, after the grooms have gone for the night. We will have to go on horseback."

"What shall I bring?"

"As little as possible. Once we are safely away, I will buy you whatever you need. You may be able to send for your things later…" His words linger.

I know why he hesitates. Because he honestly doesn't know if that will be a possibility. He once compared me to Helen and himself to Paris, now here we were, risking everything for a chance at happiness, for our love—just as they had. There is a real possibility that it may cause an irreparable rift not just between our families and the empress, but between our nations as well. A new Trojan war.

I can only pray we will meet a kinder fate then those Greek lovers.

I hurry back to my room and sit on the end of the bed anxiously. The maids come and I send them away, feigning a headache. Once they are gone, I take my mother's smallest trunk and topple it on my bed. I stuff the clothes under the covers and pull the blankets up high. Then I take my two favorite gowns, the jewels Mother gave me, and one of the empress' pins, a pearl snowflake, and set them inside. I set the rest of the gifts out on my table, admittedly sad to leave them behind. I loosen my hair and retie the simple white ribbon.

Then I take a seat in my open window and watch the stars glisten in the sky as I wait.

As soon as the first bell chimes midnight, I light a candle and grab my small case, sneaking as quietly as I can out my door. I hurry down the hall and to the grand staircase, now empty in the middle of the night. In the ballroom, I can hear the maids cleaning after the dance so I double back, going the long way around to avoid being seen. When I push the door open and step outside, I take a deep breath. The air is cool and crisp and holds the promise of freedom. I hurry across the grass to the stable where a single light flickers inside.

As soon as I slide open the stable door, my heart sinks.

Chapter FIFTEEN

Standing there in the glow of the lantern in the empress, still in her gown from the feast. There are two guards holding Alexander, who has been tied up and gagged. I cry out and reach for him, but the empress grabs a riding crop from the wall and slaps me across the arm with it in one smooth, cruel motion.

"Please, let him go," I beg.

She steps between us, obscuring him from my view.

"You selfish, stupid girl. What were you thinking?"

I take a deep breath, steeling myself against her wrath.

"I love him," I say flatly, a challenge in my voice.

The empress folds her arms across her chest.

"And you were willing to throw this all away, everything I've done for you, everything I've given you, for this boy?"

"Yes," I say honestly. "Please, don't hurt him. Haven't you ever been in love?"

She flicks her hands and the guards carry him away, even as he kicks and rages against his bonds. He's trying to scream, but I can't make out his words.

Stepping forward, she grabs me by the throat, nearly lifting me off my feet.

"I offered you my country! My crown! And this is how you repay me?"

I open my mouth to beg on Alexander's behalf, but I can't draw breath. I feel sparks firing in my eyes and when she finally releases me, I fall to the straw-covered ground, gasping for breath.

"How far did this go?" she demands, her eyes wide. "Did you sacrifice your virtue to him?"

I shake my head.

She sighs. "Thank goodness for that at least. What you are going to do now is turn around and go back to your room, as if this never happened. Is that clear?"

I shake my head. "Please, don't hurt Alexander. If you tell Peter, he will kill us both. Please."

She kicks a pile of manure at me.

"You stupid girl. I won't tell Peter, but not for your sake or the sake of that ungrateful boy. My house will not suffer such indignity as this. No, you will go back to your room as I said and tomorrow you will make the engagement to Peter official. Is that clear?"

I nod furiously.

She steps forward, using the riding crop to turn my face up to her so she can look in my eyes. "And if you ever even think of doing something so stupid again, or if you breathe a word of this to anyone, I will have the boy killed. He and your entire family, and I assure you, it will be a slow, painful death. Do you understand?"

"Yes, Your Majesty."

"Good. Now go, before anyone else sees you out of bed."

I pause, picking up my trunk slowly.

"And Alexander?" I ask weakly.

She sets the crop back on its hook on the wall.

"No harm will come to the boy, so long as you keep your word."

I don't know whether I believe her or not, only that I have no choice but to comply.

She calls out after me.

"It's lucky for you that your lady saw you leaving your chamber tonight and had the good sense to come to me immediately." She sighs. "Think of the terrible mistake you so narrowly avoided."

The blood in my veins boils with rage as I return to my chamber, cursing the person responsible for sabotaging my chance at happiness, and praying the empress keeps her word.

When morning comes, the maids find me bleary-eyed and still in my gown from the previous day. They hurry me into a bath and dress me in fresh clothes; they even fuss with my hair since my ladies are conspicuously absent. I can't help but wonder which of them reported me to the queen. My eyes narrow.

Of course it was Elizavetta. Rina may have seen and suspected something, but she never would have betrayed me like that. I stomp over to their room and throw open the door, only to find all their belongings gone.

Had the empress sent them away? Or something much worse? I gather myself enough to go to the library, where I pull the book from its shelf. There's nothing inside. Frantic, I begin grabbing other books, flipping through the pages, hoping for something, *anything*, that will tell me that Alexander is all right. But there's nothing. I shudder, unable to keep the image of the chancellor's bloody body from my mind. That would be a mercy compared to what Peter would do to him if he found out. I quickly write a note of my own and stick it in the pages of our book.

My eyes are dark and blind, I cannot see; to whom or whither should my darkness flee, but to that light? And who's light but thee? If I have lost my path, dear lover say, Shall I wander in a doubtful way?

I replace the book on the shelf and steady myself for a moment, trying to smother down the waves of agony rolling through me.

I don't hear anyone approach, I'm much too lost in my own pain for that.

"Ready for another lesson already?" Sergei's voice rings though the room, clear as a bell.

I turn and there is light in his face, not a trace of knowledge of my shame. Unable to help myself, I run to him, throwing my arms around his neck. He hesitates only a moment before returning my embrace, and then he sets me back softly.

"What is it? What's wrong?"

I shake my head. If the empress did not tell him, then she would have told no one. And I cannot either, less she find out and takes it out on the people I care about. I take a step back, frowning.

"I'm sorry, Sergei. I only just realized that I am very alone here."

He tilts his head to the side.

"Not alone. You have me."

I bite my bottom lip. "No, I cannot have you. Don't you see? I can't care for you without putting you in danger. I can't care for anyone."

He lowers his chin and whispers, "You needn't fear Peter's wrath. I can handle that much, I assure you."

"Today I become his, his property and possession. There is nothing else for me in this life."

Reaching out, Sergei takes my hand, but I pull away. If there were even the slightest whisper of impropriety now, with Sergei or anyone at all, the empress would have Alexander's head, of that I have no doubt.

"Who is this small, broken girl in front of me? Where is the fearless young woman I beheld, standing in the snow, knife in hand, ready to fight to her last breath?"

I frown.

"She's gone. Killed by this place."

He shakes his head. "No, I don't think so. You, Sophie, are a fighter. Don't stop fighting now. I know things seem dark, but that is when you must fight the hardest."

"What if I have nothing left to fight for?" I say, my voice shaking.

"Then you fight until you find something to fight for. But the moment you stop fighting the current, the moment you surrender to it, that's when you are truly lost."

What can I say to make him understand that I'm already lost? My heart and soul, the very core of me, has been taken—I'm nothing but a shell now. Peter and the empress… I think I hate them. I think I truly hate them both.

As if reading the anger stirring inside me, Sergei lowers his head and whispers, "Don't let them break you, Sophie. Don't let them win."

His words echo in my mind. I straighten myself, brushing my hands along my skirts and squaring my shoulders. I pull myself up as tall as I can and take a deep, calming breath.

"You're right, of course," I say coldly.

The air around me changes, or perhaps I only imagine it does. The thick, clouded feelings thin and melt away, leaving a clear path in front of me. I will do what I can to save Alexander, to save my family. I will please the empress and learn to bend Peter to my will. I will wear the crown of Russia, secure my father's lands, and my brother's title. These things, at least, are within my power.

I bow my head and take my leave, heading to the one person who might be able to help me achieve my goals.

Tapping lightly on the door, I wait until she calls me in.

"Madame Groot," I say pleasantly.

She curtsies and waves for me to sit.

"I'm sorry to disturb you, but I find myself in need of your counsel."

"Of course, dear," she offers, ringing for the maid.

"Bring us some tea, please," she orders the young girl.

"Actually, vodka for me, if you please," I interject.

If she's surprised by my request, she hides it well.

"So," Madame Groot says curiously. "What brings you to me today?"

I hold myself rigid as we speak.

"The empress plans to announce my engagement to Peter today," I say. She nods, unmoved by my confession.

"As you may suspect, Peter can be…" I try to think of a diplomatic way to put it, "difficult at times. He needs someone who can encourage him toward the right decisions."

She tries to hold back a sly grin, but I see it before she can control her expression.

"And you would like me to help teach you methods of encouragement?"

I nod.

"Yes. My mother had a similar temperament. Often my father would have to gently persuade her to his way of thinking. It is a subtle art, a skill which I do not possess."

The maid returns with a pot of tea and a tall bottle of vodka. Madame Groot pours me a glass of the clear alcohol, then one for herself, abandoning the tea altogether.

"Of course I can assist you with this. I'm actually quite pleased you thought to come to me with this. Many girls are content to bend to their lovers' will—few have the courage to learn the art of bending him to theirs."

I take a drink, trying to sip it slowly as it burns my mouth for a moment before sliding like warm honey down my throat.

We talk and drink as she walks me through a series of exercises. Some are techniques of subtle seduction, how to draw his attention by subtly touching your neck or shoulder, ways to look meek while still alluring. Other things are subtle verbal tricks, how to lead someone to a conclusion by offering small hints of phrase or how to use their own words to twist their thoughts in another direction.

Everything she says I store away in my mind like weapons, to be used when I need them.

"And specifically in Peter's case," she adds finally, "cruelty can never be met with cruelty. If he is feeling in any way attacked, he will lash out like a wounded animal. When he is angry or cruel, you must remain calm, pliant even. Offer him kindness—or at the very least indifference—to cool his temper."

A thought occurs to me.

"Madame, did you tutor Peter as well?"

The light in her eyes dies just a bit, and she nods sadly.

"I did. He came to me as a young man. He was cocky and arrogant, as many noble boys can be. I taught him to be charming, to smile and flatter. I hoped he might use those tools to become a better man, but instead he uses them like a mask. He flirts and he fawns, but I think deep down, there is a darkness in him."

I take a slow breath, holding my expression neutral.

She continues, "It's not the boy's fault, not really. The empress brought him here and lavished gifts and riches upon him like a little prince. But what she never gave him was time, never gave him real affection. So he grew up as a spoiled, but unloved, boy. He never learned how to receive affection, how could he possibly be expected to know how to give it to someone else?"

I take another drink, refusing to allow myself to feel pity for him.

"But the empress seems to have genuine affection for you," she offers with a smile.

I raise one eyebrow but say nothing. If the empress loved me at all, she had a very strange way of showing it. Perhaps that's what had broken Peter. If this is how she treated someone she loved, how must she have treated someone she didn't love? I force the thought away.

"Thank you for the lesson, I am deeply grateful," I say, setting down my empty glass. "But I must go prepare for tonight."

She nods and takes my hands.

"My door is always open to you, dear Sophie."

I tense, feeling the muscles in my back go rigid as I respond flatly.

"It's Catherine, now."

Chapter Sixteen

When I return to my room, a gift from the empress is waiting for me. A large, sky blue box with a silver bow. For a terrible moment, I wonder it Alexander's head is inside. My fingers tremble as I pull away the ribbon and lift the lid. Inside are two golden, oval frames, one holding a painting of myself, the other a painting of Peter. The frames are inlaid with diamonds and rubies. I stare at his image; the artist certainly captured his mischievous smile, the squint of his eyes, even the soft wave of his golden hair. I feel the anger rising up inside me again, and it's all I can do to hold it at bay.

My valet pushes the door open.

"The Grand Duke Peter is here for you, Princess."

I nod, and Peter steps into the room. He's dressed in his formal uniform suit, dark blue with gold buttons and embroidery. A thick, light blue sash crosses his chest, covered in medals and pins of the finest jewels.

He bows deeply.

"Princess, you look lovely today."

I curtsy.

"I would say the same, Peter. You look like such a handsome general; I fear I will pale in comparison standing next to you."

He grins at the flattery.

"My ladies seem to have disappeared today," I complain. "Would you be so kind as to help me into my jewels?"

He bows his head and I take him by the arm, leading him into my private room, where everything is laid out on the table as I'd left it.

"Would you mind helping me choose what to wear?" I ask softly.

He steps forward, picking up the tiara he gave me and setting it on my head. Then he chooses the diamond necklace and one pin, affixing it to my own blue sash. Though the jewels are minimal compared to what he's wearing, I offer him a flirtatious smile, which he returns warmly.

"Are you nervous?" he asks, leading me back to the outer chamber.

"A bit," I say sheepishly. "My stomach is in knots."

That's true. My stomach is rolling like a ship at sea, but not because I'm excited, only because I'm anxious to see if the empress has kept her word, and kept Alexander safe. My mother steps out of her chamber in a gown very similar to mine, and offer Peter a formal curtsy.

"My Lord," she says.

He acknowledges her briefly, turning back to me. "Don't be nervous," he says with a wink. "I will be beside you the entire time."

I try to smile, to feign encouragement at his words, but inside I can't help feeling disappointed.

Taking my arm, he leads us down the hall to where the empress waits, along with the bishop and the synod, and most of the senate, who have traveled from Moscow for the event. Sergei is there as well, right at the empress' side. He smiles at me, an expression of pride and encouragement, as he steps in line behind the empress.

Her gown is the largest I've ever seen, jutting out from her hips and accentuating her tiny waist. She wears a tall crown and the imperial mantle about her shoulders. Draped in sashes and ribbons, dripping with diamonds, she begins the procession, Peter and I behind her, my mother and Sergei behind us, and the rest of the group following them. Mikhail is there, but my ladies—and Alexander—are conspicuously absent. I almost ask Peter about him, but I can't seem to force his name past my lips. So I hold my head up, smiling softly, as we walk through the crowded halls and down the majestic staircase.

We walk through the rotunda and across the grounds, the procession flanked by guards carrying a tall, silver canopy above us as we move. The square is filled with men of the guard regiments, as well as people from the town who have come to see us and witness the news. Beside me, Peter is stoic, not a trace of humor on his face. I try to remain the same, though I do wave subtly to a group of small children as we pass, making them squeal with joy.

We reach the cathedral just as the sun begins to set behind it, illuminating the whole scene in golden light as it bounces off the tall spires. Inside, we are led down the aisle, flanked by visiting nobles on each side, and approach the red velvet-covered dais. The empress reaches out to the archbishop in his long, black robes, and sets two small rings in his hand. She then turns and takes her place to Peter's left. Our hands still clasped, we approach the archbishop and kneel at his feet.

He begins with a prayer before reading the official announcement of our engagement. He hands Peter one ring and me the other. We say our pledges—Peter in German and mine in Russian—and take turn placing the rings on each other's fingers. Another blessing is said and the archbishop steps aside, making room for Count Lestocq, who unrolls a small scroll and reads it aloud. It's an imperial decree granting me the rank of grand duchess and the title, Imperial Highness. I'm not expecting the honor so I don't look up, even when the archbishop returns, laying a hand on my head. Beside me, I feel Peter shift uncomfortably before he takes my hand again and pulls me to my feet. We turn, and the chapel erupts in cheers and clapping. The empress turns, leading us out of the cathedral and back to the palace where the musicians have already begun to play.

Long tables overflowing with food and drink fill the palace. The empress takes her place at the head of the first table, instructing Peter and I to take seats to her left and right. I quickly down a glass of wine and a plate of beef. I scan the crowd, looking for a familiar face, but find none, save Sergei, who is chatting with some of the Senators.

The empress leans over and whispers to me.

"You did well today. I have a gift for you."

I frown, trying to look humble rather than revolted.

"Thank you, but you have given me far too much already."

She claps her hands and the sea of people part. Alexander strides into the room, Rina at his side. They approach the empress and bow.

She stands, her voice silencing the masses.

"I am so pleased to announce the marriage of Alexander Mananov and Lady Ekaterina Vorontsova."

She claps, and the others in the hall applaud too. I feel my face fall into a stunned expression, quickly followed by one of abject horror, all before I can recover myself.

Peter laughs, pounding the table with his fist.

"Alexander, you dog, I had no idea."

Alexander bows his head, not looking at me.

"It happened quite quickly," he mutters.

The empress smiles down.

"Yes, they came to me only this morning, seeking my blessing, which I gave. Of course, they wished to marry immediately, and I hadn't the heart to make them wait, so I sent them off to a small chapel outside the city."

She salutes them with her glass of wine.

"To the happy couple," she says merrily.

Others join in on the toast, but I can't move. It takes every ounce of my restraint to sit there, unspeaking and unmoving, as people around me cheer. The room spins, the air becoming hot as an oven, and I have to drain my glass of wine just to stifle the heat.

Alexander finally glances up, his eyes meeting mine, and my stomach rolls painfully, threatening to return the food I just ate. His expression is neutral, though his eyes—his beautiful, green-gold eyes—swirl like the ocean. The empress waves her hand.

"Please, indulge us by leading the first dance," she commands. Alexander bows and takes Rina by the hand, leading her to the dance floor.

As soon as the empress sits back down, I lean over, opening my mouth to excuse myself back to my room. She looks over at me sharply.

"I have fulfilled my promise," she mutters, taking a drink. "He is unharmed, though he will no longer be a distraction."

I feel her words like daggers in my heart. I admit I'm relieved to see him alive but this, this is so much worse somehow. To know that she forced him to marry another, and not just anyone, but my dear friend. It's as if my heart is cracking into a million pieces, shattered glass in my chest. If a person can die from a broken heart, surely I am not long for this world.

She drops her voice to a whisper. "Now, you will fulfill your promise. You will marry Peter and give him heirs. Because if you do not, the suffering you endure this night will seem like a fond memory. Do you understand?"

I nod.

"Should you fail or falter in any way," she adds, nodding to where Rina and Alexander stand on the floor, arm in arm, "others shall pay the price."

All night, I sit at that table, trying to think of some way to speak to him, to both of them, without the empress seeing. But she's watching me like a hawk, and I dare not step a toe out of line.

When things finally begin winding down, I excuse myself to my room. By then, Peter is much too drunk to care but the empress snaps her fingers and waves to Sergei.

"Sergei, the grand duchess is tired and feeling light-headed from the wine. Would you be so kind as to escort her to her room?"

He grins and bows.

"Of course, Your Majesty. It would be my honor."

He offers me his arm, and I take it. Alexander and Rina have long since departed and I can't help wondering if they are together, sharing their marriage bed as we would have. I sicken at the thought.

I'm so lost in my morbid thoughts that I don't notice when Sergei makes a wrong turn and we end up far from my room. It's only when he pats my hand and I look up, shaken from my shallow trance, that I see where we are.

"You have ten minutes," he whispers, leaning forward and kissing my forehead softly before releasing me.

I blink and turn around. The door to the secret room looms in front of me. My hand trembles as I reach out and push it open. Alexander rushes me, pushing the door closed quickly and pulling me into his arms. I feel myself sag against him, tears coming before the relief even sets in.

"I was so worried about you," I say in a rush, pulling back so I can kiss his face. "I was so afraid she was going to have you killed."

He presses his forehead against mine, his eyes closed as if in prayer.

"She sent for Rina right after they took me away. She gave us an option, either we would marry, or she would have you killed in your sleep."

I choke on a sob.

"And she told me if I didn't marry Peter, she'd have you killed."

I'm shaking all over.

"Shhh, it's all right," he coos, holding me tightly

against him. "I'm here now."

I let him hold me only for a moment longer before I pull away, wiping my eyes with my sleeves.

"She has made it very clear what she will do to you, to both of us, if this is discovered," I say firmly. He sits on the bench, looking so helpless and defeated.

"I don't care," he whispers.

"Yes, you do. And so do I. Besides," my voice wavers, threatening to betray me, "Rina is a wonderful, kind, sweet girl. She deserves better than to be a pawn in the empress' sad little games."

He blinks up at me.

"What are you saying?"

I take a breath, forcing the air into my lungs like swallowing fire.

"I'm saying, she is your *wife*. That cannot be undone, and it cannot be ignored."

He leaps to his feet, taking my face in his hands.

"I do not love her, you know that. My heart is yours; it always has been and it always will be."

He sounds so determined, so sincere. I feel even more fissures crack in the seams of my heart, but I press on.

"You must be her husband," I say sadly. "You must love her, as best as you can. She deserves happiness, no matter how small. And so do you."

He shakes his head to protest, but I stop him with a kiss. It's soft, slow, and full of regret. When I pull away this time, he doesn't try to stop me.

"I can offer you nothing but misery and suffering. She can give you a life, a family. Don't push her away on pain of my love, for I could not bear it."

He frowns.

"And you? What will you have?"

I feel my resolve waver only for a moment, my hesitation replaced by ice and steel. I am Helen, if she had been of greater courage, and I will keep the people I love safe. Even if that means letting them go.

"I will have what I've always had, myself. And I will have a lifetime worth of sweet memories to keep me warm at night. Don't weep for me, my love. Live your life in joy, and know that if I could have lived it with you, I would have."

I turn and open the door, not looking back as I take Sergei's arm and let him lead me back to my room. I'm alone in my bed before I let the grief overtake me.

Chapter Seventeen

The weeks pass quickly after that, spring blossoming into summer like the roses outside my window. I spend my days in lessons, either with Sergei—though he tells me I'm practically fluent already—or with Madame Groot, or with the empress herself. I quickly become accustomed to sitting for hours at the banquets and balls. I dance only with Peter and only when he insists, a false smile is my shield against the never-ending pain of my loneliness. I sit in on many meeting with the senate and the synod, learning what I can. They are all impressed with my quick mind and fair judgment. I find the empress well reasoned and slow to anger, though she is also easily swayed by the seemingly endless parade of men who share her bed.

Sergei is charming as ever, his manner relaxed and playful. He never speaks of my last moments with Alexander; I don't even know how he came to bring me to the door that day. Perhaps it was Alexander himself who confided in him, but I do not bring it up. Sergei flirts, jokes, and tries to lighten the mood. Though it's hard not to respond to him, some days it feels too false, too tiring. Some days he sits next to me and reads, and I close my eyes, letting the timber of his voice carry me away like leaves on the wind. Those are the only times I feel even half alive, and his company is my only respite.

The chancellor is reinstated, at the empress' behest. And though he still bears the scars of Peter's abuse, he seems to remember as clearly my kindness and has become my ardent defender.

Peter's moods are ever inconsistent. One day, he seems to have nothing to do with me at all. The next, he refuses to leave my side. He even sneaks a kiss once in a while, which I don't discourage. I simply close my eyes and pretend he is someone else.

I do not speak to Alexander, except when absolutely necessary in polite company. I don't look inside our book or visit our secret room. I try very hard not to think of his touch, not even in my dreams, which often betray me with visions of his face.

The empress busies herself making plans for our wedding, and thankfully asks little of me other than the occasional opinion on food or music. She has me moved into Peter's wing, the hall of the grand duke and duchess. I have new ladies and maids, and we often wile away the evenings with games and cards. She even brings in a dance instructor, a short, slender Frenchman named Pierre, to teach us all the latest dances from Paris in preparation for the wedding.

Gifts from the empress keep arriving, nearly daily. Gold, silver, and diamonds. Most of it I send back to my father, some I keep for new gowns and ribbons, some I even send to Mother, who had been indisposed on her way home, extending her stay in King Frederick's court.

Operas, plays, and dances buzz through the palace every night in an unyielding event of gaiety. I, however, can barely tolerate them. Finally tired of the noise, I wake up early one day and have an archery station erected in the meadow. I once thought to use it as a ploy to catch Peter's attention, but now I instruct the whole thing be kept as quiet as possible, so as not to draw his notice.

As I stand in the meadow, releasing one arrow after another, only my silent maid Henrietta accompanying me, I feel the wind rush through my hair and I can relax. Each arrow that flies carries a piece of me away with it until I'm numb from everything.

"May I join you, Your Highness?" a familiar voice asks. I look over my shoulder and see Rina walking toward me, her golden hair blowing softly in the breeze.

I relax my arm, lowering the bow.

"Of course. It's good to see you, Rina."

She tilts her head.

"And you, we haven't spoken in some time."

I nod and dismiss my maid, sending her off to the

kitchen for some water.

"How have you been?" she asks, gently.

I frown.

"Busy. There's always so much to be done."

She nods, looking over her shoulder to be sure the maid has gone.

"I just wanted to apologize," she begins, but I stop her, raising my hand.

"No, it is I who am sorry. You were dragged into this because of me. I know you did what you did for fear for my life, and at your queen's order. I do not blame you. I never did."

She walks closer, handing me an arrow.

"Yet, you avoid me, even with your eyes."

I take the arrow and tap it against my chest.

"It's not you who I avoid. But I think it is best if I keep my distance. It is not I, but the people close to me who suffer for my mistakes."

She reaches out gently.

"I do not suffer, please don't think that. Alexander is a good man. He is kind and patient. I could not ask for a better husband."

I pat her hand, looking away quickly.

"I'm glad for that," I manage weakly.

Turning back to the target, I draw my bow, letting the arrow fly. It hits dead center.

"I would hate to be whomever you are imagining on that target," she says with a light chuckle.

"As would I," another voice calls over. Peter and

Alexander approach quickly. I feel myself stiffen as Peter rushes over, lifting me into his arms and placing a kiss on my lips. He releases me to my feet, and I look away.

"I didn't expect to see you this morning," I say. "I thought you had a meeting with the chancellor."

Peter shrugs, as if it's nothing at all, and takes the bow from my hand.

"Here, let me show you how it's done."

He takes an arrow and draws it back quickly, his form terrible, and releases it, sending it wide of the target.

"I think the wind took that one," Alexander says lightly.

I glance over briefly, watching as Rina weaves her arm though his.

Peter laughs and shoots again, this time narrowly hitting the edge of the target. Frustrated, he shoves the bow back into my hands.

"Must be warped," he grumbles.

I lift an arrow and pull it back, closing one eye as I find my target. I release the string and the arrow flies wide, landing in the distant tree with a loud thunk. I lower the bow.

"You must be right, my lord," I say flatly.

He grins, clapping his hands together.

"Let's do something else then," he suggests wildly. "Let's go for a ride. We can race through the trees; the first to the lake wins a chest full of silver!"

I glance over at Alexander, who hesitates.

"I think we shall pass on the game today," he says, one hand resting protectively over Rina's belly. I catch the gesture immediately, but it takes Peter a minute to catch on.

He laughs loudly, clapping Alexander on the back.

"Well done, you dog, well done." He turns to me, placing a heavy hand on my shoulder. "I can only hope my wife will perform as well."

I feel the blood drain from my face as I force a smile.

"Congratulations," I mumble halfheartedly.

"It looks like it's just us then," Peter says. "I'll tell the groom to ready the horses if you will go and get changed quickly."

I nod and smile, so he darts off toward the stables.

"It's not—"

I hear Alexander begin to speak so I turn my back on him quickly, grabbing another arrow and letting it fly.

It hits the target dead center, the arrow flying so hard it's halfway impaled in the hay behind it.

I set the bow down and unstrap my arm guard, dropping it at the ground at his feet as I walk past him, not looking back.

That night I'm summoned to the empress'

chambers. Sergei arrives and bids me come with him, though I am already in my nightdress.

"It's urgent, and she will not wait," he says.

Hurrying alongside him, wracking my brain to think of anything I might have done, any possible thing that might have displeased her, I nearly run to her room. The door opens and the physician is there, his expression grave.

"What, what is it?" I ask, pushing past him.

The empress is sitting in her bed. She orders everyone out, save for me. Once they are gone, I close the door and sit by her side, as she had once done for me.

"You must marry Peter right away," she says urgently, taking my hand.

I shake my head. "I don't understand. You said the spring. March..."

She frowns, clutching the blankets to her chest. "No, I've had a vision."

"A vision?" I ask clumsily.

"Yes, oh, I know how it sounds. But I was lying in bed, praying as I often do, and a vision came to me."

"A vision of what?" I ask softly, wondering if I should call the physician back in. Her cheeks are flushed, her eyes rimmed in dark circles. She looks quite frantic.

"Peter is sick."

I shake my head, "No, you're mistaken. I saw him only today. He's perfectly well."

She's too lost in her own mind to hear my words.

"He's so frail, he always has been. So sickly and small."

I frown, but take her hands.

"You must marry him now. He must have an heir."

I sigh deeply. "Even if we marry tomorrow, who knows how long it might be to conceive a child. Madame Groot says—"

She cuts me off.

"Yes, yes. Go see Groot for some herbs. She has herbs that can help with that; I've seen her give them to others."

"But," I begin, only to be cut off again.

"Next week. The wedding shall happen next week."

I nod, not knowing what else to say. I stand to leave and she grabs my arm, pulling me down roughly.

"And you will conceive—and quickly. Or else."

Her implication is clear. I nod once and leave, letting Sergei walk me back to my room in silence.

I don't bother going to Madame Groot. We have already discussed the matter. She shares the empress' concerns about Peter's health. She even suggests that because of a rather nasty bout of fever he had as a boy, that he may have great difficulty conceiving a child.

Still, it will not be seen as a failure on his part, but on mine. Wives who fail to conceive—especially royal wives—do not suffer from very long lives. Madame Groot has given me two vials of herbs, one to help conception, the other to prevent it, to be used at my discretion.

The whole affair draws my mind back to that image, scarred into my memory, of Alexander's hand on Rina's belly.

I throw myself across my bed, unable to force it away. I ball myself up, wrapping my arms around my middle, until I finally fall asleep near dawn.

At one point, a maid comes in to tell me that I have a visitor. I tell her to send them away and fall back into my slumber. When I wake again, it's nearly dinner and I know I must do my part, show up and, wearing my phony smile, pretend that everything is all right.

I can't help but hope that if I just pretend long enough, maybe one day it will be true, and I won't have to pretend any more.

My maids help me dress but before I can leave for dinner, my visitor returns.

"Rina," I say coolly, trying to remain detached from the storm of emotions hovering around me.

"Your Highness," she says with a curtsy.

"Might I have a word, privately?"

I nod and excuse my maids.

Once they are gone, I fold my hands in my lap, mentally preparing myself for whatever she wants to tell me.

"I want you to know," she begins softly, "that Alexander is a good man."

I nod, but say nothing.

"And someday, he might even grow to love me," she continues. I feel my hands begin to shake. "Maybe even as much as he loves the ghosts in his heart."

I force myself to relax, to keep my expression placid.

"And I hope so too. You deserve happiness."

"We never meant to hurt you," she whispers. "Even Elizavetta. She thought you might be in trouble; she never meant to betray you."

I stand quickly, my tolerance at its level.

"If you believe that, then you are a fool. Elizavetta has wanted nothing more than to hurt me since she arrived, and on that, you can compliment her on a job well done." I pause. "And as for you and Alexander, please, keep your distance. I believe you mean well, but I cannot… it's too hard. So, if you love me, if you care for me at all, please find your happiness far away from me."

She doesn't move as I brush past her and gather my ladies, heading down to the banquet.

Chapter Eighteen

The days leading up to the wedding are frantic. I barely have time to breathe. To be honest, the distraction is welcome. Elizavetta returns to court after taking news of Rina's wedding—and a trunk full of gold to smooth things over—to their family. She's as arrogant and rude as ever, though more openly now. I ask the empress to reinstate her as my lady, not because I want her but because Sergei suggested I keep her close.

"It's easier to watch your enemies when you always have them in sight," he says.

I hear her high, nasal voice and see that mop of unruly, red curls and part of me wants to strangle the life out of her. But I smile softly, paying her antics no mind, and that seems to drive her most crazy. She takes to flirting with Peter again, which is easy enough to shrug off.

Two days before the wedding, I'm summoned to the physician's chamber. Sergei accompanies me, holding my hand the whole way. He leaves me at the door, but tells me to be brave and that he will be waiting outside.

"Don't worry, dear," the doctor says. "This is a simple thing; it will only take a moment."

Then he hands me a small vial of blue liquid.

"What is it?" I ask.

"Belladonna, just a touch, to help you relax. Drink up," he says calmly.

I obey. Pulling the cork, I quickly drink the bitter contents.

"Good, now sit here," he says, waving to a long, white lounge.

I do, and he gently pushes me back from the shoulders until I'm lying down.

"Now take slow, deep breaths and count to ten."

I do as he asks, barely aware as he starts rolling up the hem of my gown. I want to sit up, to protest, but I'm suddenly so weak that I can barely keep my eyes open. I count as far as six before the darkness washes over me. The next thing I know, Sergei is standing next to me, helping me sit up. I blink down and I'm fully dressed, though my legs are tingly and numb.

"Can you stand?" he asks.

I shake my head, and it feels like a sack of rocks.

He lifts me easily into his arms, my head rolling against his chest. He and the doctor walk into the hall, talking about me.

"Please let the empress know everything is in order. She's young and healthy. And perfectly fit for childbirth, so far as I can tell."

"I will relay that. Thank you," Sergei says.

The doctor adds, "We will check her again after the wedding, to confirm the consummation."

Sergei nods and turns away briskly.

"Are you all right?" he whispers to me as he walks.

I sigh. "I'm fine. Just tired."

He sings softly, a lullaby, as he carries me. I let my eyes close and don't open them again until I'm at my room.

The empress lets me skip dinner that night, citing stomach pain. Instead, I sit with my ladies, whose names I can scarcely remember. I'm very careful now, not to get to close to any of them, lest my affection for them be used against me later. We play cards and read until I excuse myself to my room for bed.

The next day the seamstress comes, along with the empress herself. They present me with my wedding gown. It's quite lovely, pale blue and silver and encrusted with diamonds. The bodice is cut so low that I have to ask for bits of taffeta to be added for modesty.

Four hours later, my back and legs ache and I can scarcely wait to be unbound. It's less a gown, more a torture device, and I'm thankful that I only have to wear it for one day. The nobles have all arrived, as well as the priests, cardinals, and senators. It seems as though the entire country is in attendance, making the already loud, crowded palace nearly unbearable.

As soon as I can escape, I change into my riding habit and flee for the stables. As the groom saddles my mare, I can't help wondering where I would be right now, if the empress hadn't caught us. Would we be in Sweden? Married and happy, with a child of our own on the way?

I brush the thoughts aside. Alexander has no part in my life now, as much as it pains me. I must release him from my heart. It is only then that I might be able to find some small happiness for myself in this life, carve myself a little sliver of joy to make my existence bearable.

It's funny, how I once swooned at the thought of being married to Peter, and then later was so horrified at the idea. Now, it seems somehow neutral. We are both so broken and damaged, perhaps we will find comfort in each other, perhaps our affection will grow.

I snort derisively.

Perhaps we deserve each other.

I ride off through the meadow and into the woods, much faster than I probably should. Peony is a clever horse, and she navigates the brush with ease. I ride for hours at a relentless pace, until my hands are raw from holding the reins and my behind aches. Rounding the lake, I head toward the palace, stunned when I come across a gown hanging from a low tree branch. I slowly approach the billowing skirts, a strange sound drawing my eye to the ground.

There, spread out on a wool blanket, Peter and

Elizavetta lay, tangled in each other's arms.

Peter's shirt is removed and Elizavetta wears only the thin, sheer slip from beneath her dress. Her red hair is loose and rumpled. They both turn, seeing me approach, look startled for a second, and then laugh.

For a minute, I'm too stunned to speak.

"Are you just going to sit there on your high horse and watch?" Peter bellows, making Elizavetta snicker. "Or, I suppose you could join us, if you wish," he offers with a wink.

I take a moment to compose myself, drawing back to Madame Groot's advice about meeting cruelty with kindness, or at least indifference.

I lower my head. "I'm very sorry to have interrupted, Peter, I know you are a man with," I hesitate, "physical needs. But I'm sorrier you thought that you could not come to me with them. For you, my dear future husband, my arms are always open."

Peter blinks, looking for a moment as if I've struck him with a stick. It's Elizavetta who answers crudely.

"It's not your *arms* he would have to pry open," she spits.

I take a moment to glare at her before riding forward, tugging her gown from the tree, and laying it across my lap.

I bow my head to Peter and ride off. His laughing voice follows me until I'm almost at the palace. Leaving Peony with the groom, I storm through the halls, gown in hand, until I reach Alexander's door.

I pound on the wood with my balled fist. He answers it, looking both stunned and confused as he reads the anger across my face.

"Sophie?" he asks softly.

I brush past him to where Rina sits on a lounge, sewing a tiny shirt. The sight is almost enough to make me retch. Recovering quickly, I throw the gown at her feet.

"I know my marriage isn't one of romantic intentions, but I would appreciate it greatly if you could, at the very least, try to keep your whore sister's hands off my future husband."

Her face falls, flushing with shame.

I turn to stomp by and Alexander grabs me by the arm, spinning me to face him. His green eyes are wide, his voice deep and firm.

"That's not fair. She can't control Elizavetta any more than you can—"

I pull my arm from his hand.

"Don't ever talk to me about what is fair. And don't you dare ever lay a hand on me again," I practically scream in his face.

"Or what?" he demands, folding his arms across his chest.

I'm so angry that I don't know if I want to slap him in the face or grab him and kiss him until he can't breathe. Neither seems like a good option.

He shakes his head, his dark hair falling into his eye so he has to brush it back with his fingers.

"This isn't you, Sophie. Don't let them do this, don't let them make you something you aren't."

"What do you know about what I am or am not?" I challenge.

He sighs. "I know you. You aren't cruel, never that."

I step back, realizing I'm no better than Elizavetta, standing here, coveting a man who is not mine, a man who belongs to another. I feel my chest begin to cave in, and I know I have to get out of there before I lose my mind.

I lower my eyes, looking back over my shoulder at Rina.

"I'm sorry," I manage in barely a whisper.

I rush out of the room, holding my breath until I'm far away and the sound of his slamming door hits me like a nail in my heart. Only then, do I slow down and take a breath. Closing my eyes, I begin recovering my strength, rebuilding the wall I've so carefully erected around my heart. Eventually, the pain fades, replaced by the ice-cold resolution to find something, anything, that I can hold onto here.

Passing the library on the way back to my rooms, I feel my feet slow, against my will, and turn inward. I know I should not do this, but I move, as if in a trance, and take the book from its shelf. There is a note inside. The ink is smudged, the paper obviously months old, folded and unfolded many times by the look of it.

My path is lost, my wandering steps do stray; I cannot go, nor can I safely stay; whom should I seek but thee, my path, my way?

I consider igniting the paper, but think better of it, stuffing it inside my sleeve instead. Taking a quill and paper from the table, I scribble my reply.

Hence Cupid! With your cheating toys, your real griefs, and painted joys, your pleasure which itself destroys. Lovers, like men in fevers, burn and rave, and only what will injure them do crave.

I fold it once and place it in the book, returning it to the shelf.

I turn around and am momentarily shocked to see the empress, her cold, blue eyes fixed on me.

Chapter NINETEEN

"A little light reading to ease your nerves?" she asks, circling the table and sitting on one of the tall, red velvet chairs.

I nod, trying to force a smile and failing miserably.

"I assume tour lessons with Madame Groot have gone well?"

I nod again, this time taking a seat of my own.

"Yes, Your Majesty."

"Good. Then hopefully you will have no trouble producing an heir right away. The physician tells me you are fit enough."

"Yes, Your Majesty. But Peter—"

She cuts me off.

"Peter will be fine. Men play such a small, simple role in the matter after all. We do all the hard work." She smiles slyly.

I bow my head, not wanting to anger her.

"This wedding planning has been so taxing on me," she complains, drawing on the wooden table with her finger. "I'm going to take a vacation after it's done, go to Kiev with Bestuzhev."

"That sounds lovely," I say honestly.

She puckers, her expression like a viper preparing to strike.

"I had hoped Sergei would join me as well, but he seems to think he would be better served joining you and Peter at Oranienbaum, where you will set up your own court. Do you agree?"

I frown. The idea of being without Sergei sits like a stone in my heart, but I know that if the empress suspects I have any affection for him at all, she will use it against me.

"I admit, I have never held a court of my own, but surely, Sergei would rather join you, and I can manage without him."

Her face softens.

"Well, he is quite skilled at planning and arranging things. He would probably be more useful to you. Though I'm sure being so far from me will be very difficult for him."

I nod solemnly. "I'm sure it will."

"And young Alexander and his wife have asked to be released from court, to travel back to his homeland for the birth of their child. What is your opinion on the matter?"

Her eyes are narrowed, eagerly awaiting my reaction. I try not to react at all.

With an indifferent flicker of my hand, I answer.

"Let them stay or go as you wish, it is of no matter

to me."

"Does seeing them together make you unhappy?" she prods, unwilling to let the matter drop.

I lean forward.

"Happiness and unhappiness are in the heart and spirit of each of us at times. But I think that if one feels unhappy, they need only resign to set themselves above it. To make it so that their happiness is not dependent on any one thing… or person," I add simply. "It was Your Majesty that taught me that, and I have learned the lesson well."

She sits back, impressed.

"Yes, I see that you have."

"Come to my room tonight, so that you might sit for the painter before the wedding. Skip the feast and straight to bed after. Tomorrow will be a very long day," she orders, standing and taking her leave of me.

As she requested, I dress in my yellow gown, her favorite, adorning myself with my sash and jewels, and make my way to her chambers. There are two painters, each with their own canvas, Sergei, Bestuzhev, and a few other generals and cardinals gathered in the room. They are all whispering furiously when I walk in. Slowly, all their heads turn my way, their voices going silent as they stare.

"Where shall I sit?" I ask, and though no one answers, I feel the weight of their eyes on me. Refusing to let nerves get the better of me, I cross the room to where two empty chairs sit across from the artists, and take a seat, folding my hands in my lap. The door opens again and a mop of blond hair bounds though the door, straightening his jacket. Through the crowd, I first think its Peter, only when he gets closer do I see that it's Mikhail in Peter's suit.

"Mikhail?" I ask, confused. "Where is Peter?"

Mikhail coughs, flipping his hair back.

"His Highness had other things to do this evening. He asked me to come and sit for him." The empress, who has just arrived, lowers her chin and glares at the boy.

"He asked me to sit until it is nearly done, then he will come on the morrow so they can finish his face."

The expression on her face is truly frightening. If Peter were not her only heir, I might have feared for him. Finally, she nods, giving her consent for the painters to begin.

We sit for hours, long after the lamps are lit, taking small breaks for food and drinks. Around me, the heads of state chat idly about everything from taxes to the serfs to the treaty with Prussia. I comment, when asked to, in my newly perfected Russian. As I've been trained to, I smile warmly, offering the occasional flirtatious eyelash bat or coy tilt of the head. Sergei looks on proudly, the empress, however, looks a bit put out to find herself—for possibly the first time ever—not at the center of attention.

By the end of the night, I have several requests for audience at Oranienbaum Place and even more promises of lavish wedding gifts. When I finally leave on Sergei's arm, I'm so exhausted that I can barely stand and my head is light from all the wine.

"You were radiant tonight," he offers.

I grin. "Thank you. I have had excellent instructors."

We are nearly back to my room when I sigh deeply. I would give anything to wake up and be back in Germany, at my small palace surrounded by chickens and goats. Without a thought, I touch my bodice, where a small pouch of German soil sits between my breasts—a constant reminder of what I have lost, what I have sacrificed to be in this place. If I had the whole thing to do over again, I wonder, would I change any of it? Would I go back and spare myself the pain, by denying myself my brief joy? No, I do not think that I would. But somehow, knowing what my choice would have been, had it ever been mine, is a small comfort.

"What is it?" he asks, as if somehow sensing my distress.

"I feel a bit anxious suddenly," I admit.

He takes my hand, rubbing small circles into my palm with his thumb.

"That is to be expected of any bride to be."

I shake my head. "I feel less like an anxious bride and more like a criminal about to sign my own death warrant."

I stop, realizing what I've said.

"Oh, I'm sorry. I shouldn't have said that."

Sergei stops, taking my shoulders so that I'm

facing him.

"Never apologize for speaking your feelings to me, Your Grace. But take comfort in this; I will never let anyone harm you. Not Peter or his aunt or anyone else who might be lurking in the shadows. You will outlive them all, I will personally see to it."

I stare up at him. There's such sincerity in his words, such devotion, that I can feel the warmth of it all the way to my toes.

"Sergei. My champion."

He takes my hand, kissing it softly, his eyes never leaving my face.

"Do I have your heart, as well, my dear Sergei?" I ask. It's a bold, brash thing to say, but I have to know. We have more than a passing flirtation, that much I am sure of, but it feels safe somehow. Because I know that while I care for him deeply, he could never break my heart. For my heart rests in no one's hands but my own now.

"I am yours," he whispers, "always."

Chapter Twenty

The bells ring out endlessly beginning at dawn. I've scarcely closed my eyes before my ladies come to rouse me from my bed.

Though Elizavetta is with them, I send her away, ordering her to go clean my shoes until they shine. It's a petty command, but it keeps me from having to see her face. I'm nearly dressed when my valet announces a visitor.

"Lady Ekaterina," he says to my surprise.

I nod and he waves her in. I cross over to her, taking her hands in mine. I dare not express my regret or sorrow, not with both the empress and my mother glaring at me suspiciously from across the room, so I pull her close and kiss each of her cheeks gently.

"I'm so glad you came," I say honestly.

Tears swell in her eyes and she smiles, an unspoken forgiveness that I do not deserve.

I take a step back, really letting myself look at her for the first time in months. She's pale, unnaturally so, and more slender than I remember. "Are you well?"

She frowns. "It's a normal affliction, they tell me. I can't seem to eat anything but broth and hard biscuits."

"Well," I take her hand and lead her over to the chair, motioning for her to sit, "that's because you haven't tried the wedding cake yet. The icing is made with strawberries and crème."

She smiles weakly. "I will try it to be sure."

"Do you know yet, is it a boy or a girl?" I ask curiously. "I can just see a tiny version of Alexander puttering around the palace, a tiny sword on one hand, a book of poems in the other."

"Oh, it's too soon to know for sure. I think though, that it might be a girl," she says softly.

"There's no shame in that," Mother chimes in as she fiddles with her hair. "You can always use a girl to secure your fortune. But you must, of course, try for a son immediately. Only sons are of real value."

I make a sour face that Mother cannot see, and Rina withholds a chuckle.

"We were thinking, if it is a girl," Rina pauses, licking her lips, "that we might name her Sophie."

I breathe out hard, and the maids use the opportunity to cinch up my corset more snugly than is comfortable.

"That would be lovely," I say finally, once I am able to draw a small breath again. "I'm told you are leaving court?"

She nods, "As soon as it is safe for me to travel."

I smile and hug her fiercely. "I hope you find so much joy."

When I release her, there is a gleam of unshed tears in her eyes.

"And I, you."

Once Rina takes her leave, the maids begin the tedious job of harnessing my panniers, the wide scaffolds that would hold my gown out across my hips. When they finally drape the gown over my head, I nearly collapse from the weight and Mother has to hold me upright. It's stunning, all silver brocade with gossamer roses embroidered across the skirt that seem to shimmer as I move. The empress waves to a lady, who takes a measuring tape and wraps it around my waist.

"Seventeen inches," she proclaims, and the empress nods in satisfaction.

I sit and they begin discussing how to fix my hair, what style would best hold the large crown upon my head. I catch a glimpse of it now, sitting on a red velvet pillow on the table. It's tall, thick, and covered in diamonds. When the light hits it, it scatters into a million tiny rainbows across every surface of the room. I want to be impressed, dazzled, to feel anything at all. But I'm numb, as numb as I had been on our frozen journey through Russia, only now the bitter cold isn't in my fingers and toes, but in my heart.

They decide not to powder my hair, preferring to leave it long and dark for the ceremony, adding only a slight curl and pinning it back from my face into a nest at the back of my head. The maids add the jewels, sparkling diamond raindrop earrings, bracelets, rings, and brooches. They add a little rouge to my cheeks and lips, and then I stand for my appraisal. I feel my legs shake, not from any measure of excitement, but from the sheer weight piled upon me.

The empress looks overjoyed. Lifting the crown off its pillow, she rests it upon my head. Then the maids hand her and my mother a long, silver lace train, which they affix to the shoulders of my gown.

At noon, Peter arrives in a suit made of the same fabric as my gown, and while the silver is lovely on me, it only pales him, giving his skin a sickly blue tint. He, too, is saturated in jewels—everything from the hilt of his sword to the tips of his pointy shoes is covered in diamonds. His face, normally so cheerful, is bland, as if he, too, is suffering from a lack of enthusiasm.

He doesn't smile at me as he holds out his hand, which I take, and begins to follow the empress out of the room. As we weave through the halls and descend the stairs, others join us. I watch from the corner of my eye as we pass Rina and Alexander. They smile at me with sad eyes, but I do not respond. I cannot falter now, nor allow any momentary sliver of feeling to enter my thoughts. This is not my wedding, but my gauntlet, my trial by fire. If I survive today, then, perhaps, I can begin once more to seek out some small measure of happiness.

When we reach the doors, the trumpets sound, announcing the beginning of the royal wedding procession. The sound startles me just a little, and I twitch. Peter turns, looking at me for the first time, and winks quickly.

The empress leads us to the first of twenty-four dazzling white carriages, each pulled by eight white horses, which will carry us from the Winter Palace, down Nevisky Prospect, to the Cathedral of Our Lady of Kazan, where the ceremony will take place. As the empress steps into the massive carriage, I can't help but notice the elaborate carvings etched into the sides. One, in particular, catches my eye. It's a large, wooden horse standing outside a city gate. A depiction of the fall of Troy—the last stand of Helen and her beloved Paris.

How fitting.

When we reach the cathedral, those behind us depart first, leaving us to wait as they fill their seats. When we finally enter through the massive, ivory pillars, all I can see is a sea of jeweled icons, flickering candles, and puffs of smoke from burning frankincense. All around me are faces, some familiar, some foreign, and all eyes are fixed to my face.

Peter and I approach the alter slowly, hand in hand. At one point, he gives it a reassuring squeeze, which I return. Perhaps love is not part of our destiny, but I take small comfort that there may be, at least, an understanding. That there remains an opportunity for friendship between us.

I fight to keep my feet under me as we walk, finding myself leaning on him heavily. The gown is hot and heavy and the crown is making my head and neck ache. I hear very little of what the bishop says, focusing only on keeping my breathing steady, my face serene. He chants, and we join in.

Hymns are sung, candles lit, all adding to my general discomfort.

As he speaks holy words over us, I silently pray, either for the strength to make it through this day, or for the grace of God to strike me down where I stand. When we exchange rings, I notice that he's chosen a smaller, more humble ring than I expected. It's a ruby cut in a square, surrounded by smaller diamonds. As he slips it on my finger, I wonder if he chose it himself, or if the empress had a hand in it. And then I wonder to myself if it matters either way.

The ceremony lasts nearly four torturous hours. When it finally ends, Peter and I exit back to the carriage, followed by the empress.

I begin to lift the crown from my head, and she stops me.

"Leave it," she commands.

"Please, Your Majesty, my head aches terribly."

She frowns, glaring at me. "Heavy is the head which wears the crown."

I sigh and sit back, closing my eyes.

Back at the palace, they have arranged for a ballet,

then a feast, then a ball. Peter never releases my hand, even as we enter the theater and take our seats. It takes me a while to reconcile his expression. I might have mistaken it for anger, had I never seen his anger before. But this is something quite different.

He is nervous.

I smile sweetly, hoping he sees. If he does, his expression remains unchanged.

Finally, at dinner, I can barely open my eyes. The ache in my head has grown into a constant, relentless pounding so strong it turns my stomach. Luckily, I don't have to wait long. The empress stands, announcing that Peter and I are to retire to our wedding bed, causing great cheers around us. The empress again leads a procession down the hall, much smaller this time, only Peter's men, my mother, and my ladies following us.

It's only now that my nerves overtake me. My stomach flutters as if full of bees and my hands shake. I had been so confident, so ready to take this step with Alexander. I could have lost myself and allowed our passion to override my judgment. I think now that it must be my one regret—that I was never with him in that way. Because the idea of holding Peter in such a tender embrace makes me feel ill.

Hand in hand, once again Peter and I walk to our new apartments, in a new wing of the palace, which consists of four large, extremely elegant rooms. One sitting room, which splits into two side chambers, both of which connected to a bedroom in the rear. They make the room I first had in the palace seem like little more than maid quarters.

Large, silver tapestries cover the walls and scarlet velvet trimmed in silver adorns every piece of furniture. There are huge, silver-gilt mirrors, and every manner of finery. The bedroom is the same in color and finery, a huge, gold-and-silver bed with the image of a large, golden crown at the head. Once in the bedroom, Peter and I split, his men follow him to his chamber, the empress, my mother, and my ladies follow me to mine. The empress removes a long, sheer pink nightdress from an oak trunk. It has no lace or frills, but even so, is shocking in its beauty.

"I had this brought from Paris," she offers excitedly. "They are all the rage in Versailles."

As my ladies unlace my corset and unstrap my heavy panniers, relief washes over me. I can breathe again, and for the first time all day, I feel the cold fog in my mind lift.

I know what to do. I'd had enough lessons with Madame Groot to be at least comfortable in my practical knowledge of how this will happen. The empress watches me, her cold eyes reminding me what is at stake now.

I must produce an heir, and quickly. Should I fail in this, she will make me suffer, make the people I care about suffer. To her, it is a matter of practicality. But I hold her gaze, knowing I will never forget her cruelty, and I will never forgive it either.

They brush out my hair and lead me back to the main bedchamber, tucking me in bed. Soon, Peter's men depart his chamber, though Peter is not with them, and the group exits. Alexander does not look back at me, lying in my wedding bed, and for that, I'm strangely grateful.

Soon, my anxiety cools into boredom. I watch as the candles burn down, straining to hear Peter's footsteps or even his breathing behind the large, oak door that separates us. Finally, I drift off, only to be startled awake when that door slams open.

I sit up, clutching the covers to my chest. Peter is glaring at me, his blond hair disheveled, his face flushed. The smell of vodka hits me the moment he steps into the room.

He points at me. "You filthy whore."

Startled, I straighten.

"Excuse me?"

He rounds the bed, pouring a glass of wine from the table.

"I should have sent you away the moment you arrived." He falls onto the edge of the massive bed, barely able to sit upright.

He's slurring his words, barely coherent. I slip out of bed slowly, walking around to him with my hips swaying, the way I'd been taught.

"Please, husband, come to bed."

I reach out to him, and he slaps my hand away so

hard that I cry out.

"Don't call me that. You are no wife of mine."

I hug myself tightly.

"Please, tell me the source of your anger, and I am sure I can put your mind at ease."

Lifting the wineglass, he throws it, narrowly missing me, and it shatters against the far wall. "Did you think I wouldn't find out?" He stands, grabs the entire wine bottle, and throws it in the same manner. "He was my dearest friend, and you whored yourself with him!"

I shake my head. "I do not know who has filled you with such lies—"

He cuts me off.

"The only person who loves me in this entire damn country, Elizavetta. She told me the truth of it. That you were going to run away with him? That you would rather have him in disgrace than rule Russia as my wife? If I had known of this betrayal sooner, I would have had you flogged!"

I feel my face harden. Curse that red-haired trollop. I would see her head on a pike for this.

"I assure you, nothing happened with Alexander. Even the court physician tested my virtue—"

"At my aunt's insistence. Because she knew of your shame!"

I struggle to hold my composure. Trying to think of what I can say that will calm his temper, but there is nothing, no comfort I can offer him.

"I love her," he says plainly. "I love Elizavetta, and I will have her as my wife."

My patience flees like a shadow chased away by the sun, and I lash out.

"What's done is done, Peter. I am your wife now, and there is no changing that. All I can offer is a fresh beginning, for both of us. If you love her, I will… be understanding of that. But make no mistake; she cannot be your wife, not so long as I'm alive."

He lowers his chin. Approaching me quickly, he grabs me by the throat.

"Then I will just have to kill you," he says with a wicked smile.

"The empress will never forgive you," I gasp. "She will declare you mad and choose another heir."

Just as the darkness creeps into my vision and I'm sure he has killed me, he releases me and I fall to my knees, gasping.

"You are right about that much at least. She has no love for me. Only Elizavetta loves me."

I reach forward, putting a hand on his leg.

"I could grow to love you, Peter. If we could find a way to be kind to each other…"

He looks down at me and for a moment, I think I see his face soften, then he kicks out, catching me in the shoulder, and sends me flying backwards. I curl up quickly, afraid he will attack me again.

"No, you are unworthy of me. This is what will happen now. I will not touch you, not this night or any other. I will continue my liaisons with Elizavetta. In a few months, I will go to my aunt, and explain to her that, despite my best husbandly efforts, you are surely barren and unable to provide the heir she so desperately needs. I will have you set aside, sent to a convent for the rest of your life, and then I will take Elizavetta as my wife."

I'm so appalled that I can't speak. Not because of his cruelty, but because of the wisdom in his plan. He could do it; he could have me declared barren. Though I doubt the empress would go to the effort to send me to a convent. She would just have me killed. But not before punishing me in any way she can think of for disappointing her.

I feel the tears slide from my eyes as he laughs and crawls into bed. He barely makes it under the covers before he passes out cold.

For a while, I just sit on the cold, stone floor, gasping for breath between sobs. What could I do now? What was I left with?

I find my feet and stagger to my window, throwing it open so the breeze can blow in. I glance over my shoulder at Peter. He's snoring loudly in his drunken stupor. I had hoped we could at least be friends, but I see now that is impossible. We will be bitter rivals, enemies sharing the same cold bed, until one of us is dead. As I stare at his face, peaceful in slumber, I wonder if I could do it. If I could press a pillow over his face until—

No. I shake the thought away.

Don't let them make you something that you're not. Alexander's words echo through my mind.

I swallow and turn back to the window, my heart heavy with thoughts of my bleak future.

Then I see him, crossing the meadow in the darkness, like an answer to my prayers. Perhaps, there is a solution after all. Perhaps, there is still hope for me yet.

Chapter TWENTY-ONE

I throw on a long, white cloak from the wardrobe in my chamber and creep from the apartment. The noise from the party floors below covers my escape. I keep the hood low, my chin down, as I race through the halls. My heart races, a new vision appearing in my mind, a vision where I find my speck of happiness, where not only do I survive this dangerous game, but I am the victor.

My feet are bare on the stone floor as I head for the back entrance of the palace, waiting in a dark alcove until I see him enter, slinking in from the shadows. His dark hair is tousled, but in a handsome way, the stubble along his jaw freshly trimmed. As he passes, I reach out and grab his arm, drawing him into the darkness with me.

At first, he's startled, then concerned.

"Sophie, are you all right? What are you doing out here?"

I pull him close as a maid passes, not seeing us.

"Sergei, I saw you from my window. Please, I need

to speak with you privately. It's urgent."

He blinks, and then checks to make sure the coast is clear before leading me off to the south corridor, to an empty bedroom.

"What has happened?" he asks, taking my hands.

"Peter is in love with Elizavetta," I say flatly. "He wants me to be declared barren and sent away so he can marry her."

His face fills with confusion, then, as he works through what I've said, he frowns.

"What do you need from me? Should I fetch Alexander?" he asks, his voice tight with resignation.

I shake my head slowly. Alexander is married—and to my dear friend—with a child on the way. Perhaps it was not the life he hoped for once, but there is joy in it for him, and I would not take it from him for anything.

"I was not thinking of Alexander," I answer slowly.

I reach up, taking the cord that fastens the cloak around my neck and tugging at it, letting it fall in a white pool at my feet. Standing there, the only light in the room coming from the bright moonlight streaming through the windows, in just my pink gown, I stretch my neck, showing him the marks where Peter put his hands on me.

With a gasp, he steps forward, touching my neck with just the tips of his fingers.

"Sergei, my champion, you told me once that I might find some small measure of joy in this life. And

I know you are right. I feel it when we are together. When I see you, my heart feels safe. You are the only man I trust completely, the only man I wish to be with this night."

I look up at him, allowing the truth of my words to fill my voice and shine in my eyes.

"Tell me, Sergei, will you do this for me?"

His eyelids lower just a bit, his breathing heavy.

"I have loved you since the first moment I saw you, my clever, brave Snow Queen."

I smile slyly. I cannot imagine a better man to have in my arms or at my side as I continue on this dangerous journey. And if it should be his child who someday sits on the throne of Russia, how much better the place would be for it.

"Then kiss me now. Let this night be the beginning of our joy," I ask, wrapping my arms around his neck.

He says nothing, but lowers his lips to mine, his stubble scratching at my face pleasantly. I feel a warmth spreading inside me, a slow boil under my skin. His kisses begin gently, but become increasingly urgent. His hand slides up my back and into my hair and I let go, losing myself in the feel of his hands, the scent of his skin like fresh pine. A familiar ache grows in my belly, and I know that there will be no pain this night—there is far too much else to feel. He lifts me, carrying me to the bed, where he sets me gently.

"Are you certain?" he asks, his voice hard, as though barely able to contain itself.

I nod and pull him to me. The last of his restraint gone, he begins to undress as I watch him, stopping him occasionally to run a hand along the muscles rippling in his stomach, back, and shoulders. When he is finally free of his clothes, he turns his full attention to me. The boil inside me becomes a torrent of pleasure and pain, and I feel myself writhe with his every touch.

Hours later, I lay in his arms, safe and content in a way I have never felt before. He traces my belly button with his finger.

"You should get back to your room before the sun rises," he whispers.

I take his hand in mine.

"Only if you make me a promise," I challenge.

He smiles, kissing my neck. "Anything."

"Promise me that you will never leave me," I say earnestly. Now that I've given myself to him, to my feelings for him, I never want to lose him. I never want to be alone again.

"I promise. Tomorrow, when you leave for Oranienbaum, I will be right there at your side. And every day after that."

"And every night?" I ask coyly.

His answer is a deep, long kiss.

By the time the sun rises, I'm back in my nuptial

apartment, packing my trunks. Peter wakes with a grunt as his servants arrive to get him dressed. I'm already bathed and in my yellow gown.

"Wake up, husband," I say merrily as our breakfast is brought in.

He groans, staring at me with one eye open.

"Your aunt will be here soon. And the maids need to make the bed."

He rolls out of bed, holding his head in one hand.

"Why are you so cheerful?" he demands. "I've not forgotten our conversation last night."

I smile sweetly. "I know, and I'm sorry you feel that way. But I thought that perhaps, after what happened between us later in the evening, that you had reconsidered your plan."

He looks confused. I point to the bed he's just vacated, and to the small bloodstain on the sheets.

"I didn't..." he stammers. "We never—"

I hold up a hand. "I know you were quite intoxicated, but don't worry, I thoroughly enjoyed myself." I put my hands on my belly. "And who knows, perhaps we already have a little prince or princess on the way."

I turn to Elizavetta, who has just come into the room. She looks at the bed in abject horror, her eyes shifting to Peter accusingly.

"Please see that those sheets are washed," I say, then blow a kiss over my shoulder to Peter, who looks as if I've struck him.

The empress rushes in behind her, ecstatic to see the bed in such disarray.

"Everything went well?" she asks pointedly.

I nod, tugging down my long sleeve to conceal the small cut in my palm I'd used to bloody the sheets.

"Everything went perfectly," I say with a wide smile. For the first time, when I look at the empress, I don't see an imposing figure or a fierce queen. I see a sad woman, terrified of losing a throne that was never rightfully hers. Her heir is a rude, cruel little boy who will never have a lick of real military or political sense. And I realize that she needs me, much more than she would like me to know. And I also realize that the power in our relationship has shifted. She must see the discovery in my eyes as I stand, unwavering, before her, because she slouches just a bit under my gaze.

I clap my hands and my ladies rush to my side, one placing my new crown upon my head. "If you'll excuse me, I have a lesson with Sergei."

I turn and walk out of the room, not bothering to look back.

The End: Book One

~Author's Note~

The true story of Catherine the Great is one fraught with betrayal, intrigue, and romance. While a good deal of my story is drawn from actual people and events, I have been very liberal in the rearrangement of dates, events, and places. Whenever possible, I took my cues from her own words, intermixing my own thoughts and ideas. My thought upon the creation of the book was simple. I looked at the woman she was when she claimed the crown and then wondered—how did an innocent girl from Germany become such a force of nature? Most people aren't born cold or ambitious, but have circumstances that forge them into those people. And that was the story I wanted to tell in this book. I wanted to see the events in her early life that would have changed her into the person she became, and not knowing the truth of that story, I simply made something up. That is what we, as writers, do best.

If you are curious about the real history behind Catherine, I suggest heading to your local library and doing a bit of research. This is not meant to be a historically accurate representation, but a flight of fancy, one that I hope you, dear reader, will enjoy as much as I have.

~Sherry

Acknowledgements

Every book is a journey, and I was very fortunate to have a wonderful group of people helping me along the way.

First and foremost is always my family. My wonderful husband and brilliant children. You guys sacrifice a lot so I can follow my dreams, and I want you to know how grateful I am for that and how much I love you all. For my extended family, my parents both blood and borrowed, my fantastic siblings and my dear cousins, I love you guys to the moon and back!

I would like to give special thanks to my publishing family over at Clean Teen Publishing. Dyan, Marya, Courtney, Rebecca, Cynthia, Melanie, and the rest of the team. You ladies make publishing a book FUN, and that speaks volumes. I have never felt so in sync with a team before, and I can't tell you how humbled and grateful I am to be working with you every day! Extra hugs and thanks to Marya for the AMAZING cover and Cynthia for being the best editor in the world!

I'd like to give a shout out to my Minion Army and the CTP street team. You guys are the best street teams a girl could ask for, and I want to thank you for all you do! You are my heroes!

Thanks as always to my beta readers, DJ, Tiffany, Amanda, and Erin. You guys are the best! Without you, my stories would linger in plot purgatory. Thanks to the hardworking bloggers who help us poor authors spread the word about our books, I would like to give you all a big hug (and I just might, fair warning. I'm a hugger).

And last but never least, thank you, dear readers, for following me on this amazing ride. I hope you all enjoy reading Sophie's story as much as I enjoyed writing it.

About the Author

Sherry D. Ficklin is a full time writer from Colorado where she lives with her husband, four kids, two dogs, and a fluctuating number of chickens and house guests. A former military brat, she loves to travel and meet new people. She can often be found browsing her local bookstore with a large white hot chocolate in one hand and a towering stack of books in the other. That is, unless she's on deadline at which time she, like the Loch Ness monster, is only seen in blurry photographs.

She is the author of The Gods of Fate Trilogy now available from Dragonfly Publishing. Her previously self-published novel After Burn: Military Brats has been acquired by Harlequin and will be released in 2014 with a second book in that series to follow. Her newest YA steampunk novel, Extracted: The Lost Imperials book 1, co-written with Tyler H. Jolley is now available everywhere books are sold and her newest YA novel, Losing Logan, is available now from Clean Teen Publishing.

CPSIA information can be obtained at www.ICGtesting.com
Printed in the USA
LVOW12s2002110914

403621LV00006B/8/P

9 781940 534909